Ruby Tanya

ROBERT SWINDELLS

CORGI YEARLING BOOKS

RUBY TANYA
A CORGI YEARLING BOOK 0 440 86398 8

First published in Great Britain by Doubleday,
an imprint of Random House Children's Books

Doubleday edition published 2004
Corgi Yearling edition published 2005

1 3 5 7 9 10 8 6 4 2

Papers used by Random House Children's Books are natural, recyclable
products made from wood grown in sustainable forests. The manufacturing
processes conform to the environmental regulations of the country of origin.

Set in Century Old Style

Corgi Yearling Books are published by Random House Children's Books,
61–63 Uxbridge Road, London W5 5SA,
a division of The Random House Group Ltd,
in Australia by Random House Australia (Pty) Ltd,
20 Alfred Street, Milsons Point, Sydney, NSW 2061, Australia,
in New Zealand by Random House New Zealand Ltd,
18 Poland Road, Glenfield, Auckland 10, New Zealand,
and in South Africa by Random House (Pty) Ltd,
Endulini, 5A Jubilee Road, Parktown 2193, South Africa

THE RANDOM HOUSE GROUP Limited Reg. No. 954009
www.kidsatrandomhouse.co.uk

A CIP catalogue record for this book is available from the British Library.

Printed and bound in Great Britain by
Cox & Wyman Ltd, Reading, Berkshire.

I'm Ruby Tanya, I've come to call for my friend Asra.

One of the men shook his head. No children play today, they have teachings, prayers.

I nodded. I know about Fridays, but the children go to school Fridays, don't they? They'd be on their way now if there'd been no bomb.

The man shrugged. If there'd been no bomb; but there was. Things are not the same.

Me and Asra are the same. Best friends, always will be.

The man smiled briefly. Your father – he knows of this friendship?

Yes. Well . . . no. I mean, I haven't told him yet . . .

To little victims everywhere
and
for Derek and Theresa Mortimer:
the years don't matter,
and neither do the miles

- One
Ruby Tanya

The bomb went off when we were all outside waiting for the prince, so that was lucky. He wasn't coming to see us: he had to drive through Tipton Lacey to get to the camp and the road goes right past the school, that's all. He was due at the camp at half past two, so he'd pass us a few minutes before. At quarter past, the teachers gave us a little flag each and lined us up along the fence, which is only three metres from the road. I felt such a plonker I wished it was three miles.

My dad loves the royals. He says they're part of what makes England the best country in the world. Mum quite likes them too, even though *her* mum's a hippy who says royalty's a rip-off. We went to Buckingham Palace loads of times when I was younger. Outside it, I mean. We never actually went *in*. We went to Sandringham too, and Windsor, and Balmoral. Dad once thumped somebody in a pub for calling the Queen a parasite. Two policemen came to the house. Mum thought they'd come to take him to prison, but they just talked to him for a few minutes. I had to go up to my room so I don't know what they said, but I was a bit disappointed when I saw them leave without him.

He's not so chuffed about today's visit though, because he doesn't like asylum seekers. At breakfast he says, What's he visiting that scruffy camp for? He'd be better off looking round the village, popping into school, seeing how packed it is now *their* brats've taken over. Dad reckons the school will start going downhill because of the asylum seekers' kids. Mum says everything'd be cool if we let real asylum seekers stay and sent economic migrants back. I try not to get involved in their fratching, it does my head in.

There weren't any asylum seekers' kids in school that afternoon, which is a shame because that's what started the trouble. They'd all got a half-day off to meet the prince at the camp.

Anyway there we were, the rest of us, lined up waiting with our little Union Jacks, and suddenly there's this terrific bang. Not *just* a bang: there was something else, something invisible that slammed me into the fence and hurt my ears and took all the air away. I didn't think, *What the heck was that?* I thought, *Maybe this is how you feel when a prince goes by.* How sad is that?

For a few seconds there was just the noise of things falling on the ground, like rain. Then the screaming started, and the shouting. I was lying on the grass with my cheek pressed up against the fence. I wasn't injured, just sort of dazed; couldn't get myself together to move my head so the fence'd stop hurting my cheek. I heard somebody – a teacher, I suppose – call out, My God look at the *school*. I didn't look. I could see across three metres of grass to the road and I saw the prince pass by. Or at least I saw his car. Long and black it was, with gleaming wheels. It didn't slow

2

down; in fact it seemed to speed up, and I bet I was the only one who spotted it.

One or two of the kids were quite badly hurt and Mr Conway the student teacher had vanished completely, but I didn't know that then.

- Two
Asra

We were very happy because the prince will visit our camp. When even a prince has seen us, spoke with us, how can they send us away? That is what my mother and all of the older people were saying. Everybody was working very hard to make the camp look nice so the prince will see we are clean people, and proud. We children have practise a song of our country to sing for him as well, though none of us wants to go back there because of the bad men.

It does not happen, this visit we all want so much, because of the explosion. The prince was coming, his motor car was very close when the explosion did damages at my school. The policemen think maybe somebody bad is trying to blow up the prince, so they turn his motor car round and hurry him away. A man comes to tell us the visit is cancelled, and also that the school will be closed tomorrow because of this explosion. He says children are hurt, a man is missing. It could be a gas explosion, or a bomb.

At six o'clock everybody is at the social club to see the TV news. The very first bit is about Tipton Lacey and it isn't gas, it was a bomb. The prince was only four hundred metres away when it went off. Two pupils have suffer perforated eardrums, a student teacher is missing. An investigation is under way. The police are having an open mind, but the possibility that this was a terrorist attack by a Muslim fundamentalist group cannot be ruled out.

We are all shocked, and also very sad. What sort of person blows up a school? What if the bomb had gone off ten minutes earlier or ten minutes later, with all the children inside?

Not *all* the children, says Mr Shofiq, our leader here at the camp. He looks worried. Not all the children were inside ten minutes earlier, and they wouldn't have been inside ten minutes later either, and that's dangerous.

Why? somebody asks. What d'you mean?

Mr Shofiq shakes his head. *Our* children, he says. None of our children was at school this afternoon. The Muslim children. No Muslim child could possibly have been in the school when the bomb exploded, or anywhere near it. They were here, every one of them. Safe and sound. I'm afraid some people are going to call that a strange coincidence.

You mean . . . ?

Yes, of course, said Mr Shofiq. We are not so popular in Tipton Lacey, are we? You mark my words: sooner or later somebody is going to suggest that perhaps *we* planted the bomb.

But why *would* we? cried the other man. We want to stay in England, make our homes here. Also it is our children's school, where they are learning English; learning to *be* English. We'd have to be insane even to *dream* of . . .

Mr Shofiq nodded. You're right, we'd have to be insane, but you see, a lot of people think that's exactly what we are:

5

mad bombers with beards and turbans. When people die, when children are hurt, people don't think. They don't take the *time* to think. The tabloids wind them up, point them in a certain direction and they go on the rampage. He shook his head. Believe me, there are dangerous times ahead. We must prepare ourselves.

I was so, so scared when Mr Shofiq said these words. I hoped he was mistaken, *prayed* that he was, but he wasn't. I suppose that's why we made him our leader.

- Three
Ruby Tanya

They took us to hospital, all forty of us plus teachers. They don't have that many ambulances so we went in relays, the most serious cases first. I was in the last batch, which was fine with me.

The hospital's in Danmouth. Danmouth Infirmary, six miles from the village. They put us in cubicles, on trolleys. After a bit a nurse came through the curtain. She smiled. What's your name, sweetheart?

Ruby Tanya Redwood.

Cool name. How you feeling?

I'm all right, but I don't know what happened. At school, I mean.

The nurse shook her head, gently turning mine to look in my ears. There was an explosion, that's all I know. Somebody mentioned a bomb but somebody always does, these days.

Follow my finger with your eyes please, Ruby.

It's not Ruby, it's Ruby Tanya.

7

Sorry, Ruby Tanya. She smiled. Sounds like *Rule Britannia*, doesn't it? You know – the song?

I sighed. Yes I *do* know, it was my dad's idea. He's a moron.

The finger moved slowly, left to right and back again. My eyes followed it. The nurse nodded. Good. Does your head ache, ears hurt?

No.

Feel dizzy at all?

No.

Nauseous?

What?

Sick; d'you feel sick, Ruby Tanya?

I said I was all right. What about the others though? Is everybody all right?

We're looking after them, don't worry. She smiled again. Doctor'll pop by soon, take a peek at you, make sure it's safe to send you home.

Mum and Dad came before the doctor, looking concerned. They fussed and twittered like they do, stroking my hair, asking where it hurt. When I told them it didn't hurt anywhere Mum burst out crying, and of course the doctor picked that moment to arrive.

When he'd calmed Mum and pulled me about a bit, he said they could take me home. I'd let her have an early night if I were you, he smiled, just to be on the safe side.

We had to pass the school on the way home. Dad slowed and wound his window down, but he couldn't see much because the police had strung blue and white plastic tape all along the fence and across the gate and there was a constable on the verge, waving everybody on. As Dad accelerated away he shouted back, It's a bit late to be guarding the place, isn't it? You tossers should be up that camp, arresting the bombers.

It scared me when he said that, because Asra lives at the camp. She's my best friend. Don't go upsetting your dad, says Mum about ten times a day, which is why I've never mentioned Asra in front of him.

He's all right, my dad, but he goes barmy when he's upset.

- Four
Ruby Tanya

I sulked about having to go to bed early. Well, I felt absolutely fine and the sun was shining and I didn't have to get up for school tomorrow: I wanted to check out the Green for lads. Then the six o'clock news came on and our bomb was the first item and it said a student teacher was missing and two pupils had perforated eardrums. If I'd known that I wouldn't have sulked, but I didn't; how could I?

Student teacher could only be Mr Conway, and missing had to mean dead. Nobody I knew had ever died before. It felt unreal. Of course I didn't *know* Mr Conway, not really, but I'd seen him around school. Thin, he was, with blond hair and a beaky, reddish nose. Kids said he was nice. Now I'd never see him again. Nobody would.

Dad?

Sssh, I'm listening.

Is perforated eardrums bad?

Dad shrugged. Dunno, love. Could be deaf, I suppose.

He looked across at Mum, who'd trained as a nurse. That right, Sarah?

Uh? Yes, could be. I think there's an operation though: implants. She looked at me. I thought you were getting ready for bed, young woman.

I *am* ready, Mum, but I want to watch.

They let me stay till the reporter handed back to the studio. In bed I snuggled down, telling myself I was lucky. What did it feel like to be suddenly deaf? Or suddenly *dead*? It was only quarter past six; it took me ages to get to sleep.

Next day was Friday. The Tipton Lacey *Star* comes out on Fridays and our copy was on the mat at breakfast time. It's a small town paper so it's not known for its sensational scoops. It usually leads with a story about wheelie bins or a giant marrow or somebody's diamond wedding anniversary, and it's all downhill from there. For once something had actually *happened* in Tipton Lacey and the editor had gone to town with a banner headline. TERRORIST BLAST HITS SCHOOL, I read upside down as Dad smoothed the paper beside his plate. Underneath in smaller print was, *One Dead, Two Critical*.

Does it say who got the whatsit eardrums, Dad – perforated?

Hang on a sec, grunted Dad. I'm reading. I watched his eyes scan the first para. Stuart, he said, without looking up. Stuart Conway was your student teacher's name. Says here he *died* in the blast so he's not missing any more, poor beggar. He was the only person inside the building at the time. He read on, then looked at me across the table.

Kelly Mountain in your class?

No, Year Five. Is she one of them?

Yes, and the other's a boy, Andrew Farrell. Know him?

11

I nodded. He's Year Five as well. It must've been where they were standing.

Dad nodded. Probably. Funny thing, blast. Blows one guy to kingdom come and leaves the feller next to him untouched.

I didn't want my cornflakes. I stared into the bowl, wondering what it'd be like to be blown to kingdom come. I felt sick, and Dad's next words didn't make me feel any better.

If I was Kelly Mountain's dad, he growled, or Andrew Farrell's, I know where I'd be right now: I'd be up at that camp with a baseball bat, waiting for the first unlucky so-and-so who stuck his nose through the gates.

What if it was a woman? murmured Mum. Or a child?

Her nose, snapped Dad. His *or* hers, it's all the same to me: one less terrorist to worry about. Pass the sugar, love, will you?

Doesn't sound like it, I know, but my dad's actually quite a reasonable guy. He's what they call easily led though, believes everything he reads in the papers, and that makes him say stupid things. *Do* stupid things sometimes. It'll land him in trouble one of these days.

- Five
Asra

Today was Friday. No; today *is* Friday. School is closed. Here at the camp I must be practising my English as if I am at school. As *if* or as *though*? It is difficult.

This camp is good because the bad men who have stolen my country can't hurt us here, but it is difficult too because of the huts. There are no houses, only the rows of huts. They are long, made of wood. Soldiers used to live in them. Mr Shofiq says thirty soldiers were living in each hut. Now each hut has four families. Blankets hanging from cords are the best we can be having for walls, to make four homes in every hut. This is not so good: everybody can hear everybody, and must walk through somebody's home to reach her own. You all come from the same country so what's wrong with that? they ask if we are complaining. Yes, we *do* come from the same country but not everybody is friends; it is the same for English people, I think. We try not to complain too much, in case they get angry and send us back to our country.

So we live always on tiptoe and whispering, waiting to be

told if we will stay or go home and be killed. The grown-ups are tense all the time: there is shouting, shoes are thrown. We children cannot do noise, we must creep like little mouses. School is better.

Before breakfast I go for a walk. To reach the door I must pass through the home of Shazad Butt. Shazad is twelve like me, but bigger. He bullies me at school. I walk fast with my eyes down, feeling his eyes following me. He would thump me and pull my plaits if he was alone, but his father is watching. I see only the floor till I close the door behind me: the Butts are none of my flipping business, as Ruby Tanya would say.

It is raining the sort of rain called drizzle, which falls a lot on England. I put my scarf over my hair and tuck the ends in my jacket. There is grass, but it is best in drizzle to keep to the concrete pathways. I walk one pathway, then another and another till I am near to the gates, which are closed. I think they are closed because nobody is going to school, but perhaps there is another reason. Four men of my country are staring through the bars at three English men on the road outside. Nobody is talking, they are just staring. I stop to watch, but one of the men turns to me. It is half past seven, he growls. Why are you not at the mess? The mess is where we all have breakfast. It is quite tidy – I don't know why it is called the mess.

I look at the man. I am going for a walk, I tell him, before breakfast.

Then walk, he says, and I walk away, wondering why the English men are here, and whether Ruby Tanya will get through the gates if she decides to call for me. I want to see Ruby Tanya, to know she's all right and to ask her about the bomb.

I could not have guessed, that Friday morning, how much the bomb was going to change our lives.

- Six
Ruby Tanya

Where are you off to? Mum asked as I zipped up my jacket. It's wet, you know.

I know, Mum, but this jacket's showerproof. I thought I'd collect my bike from school then go up the camp, call for Asra. Dad had gone to work so it was OK to mention Asra.

I'm not sure that's a good idea, Ruby Tanya. Not today.

How d'you mean? What's wrong with today?

Mum sighed. You heard your dad, love. There might be trouble. If some bunch of heroes have gone out there with baseball bats or whatever, I don't want you involved.

I won't get *involved*, will I? I'm just calling for my friend.

Yes, I know, but listen: suppose there's a reporter from the *Star*? A photographer, or even somebody from the telly? There *could* be, and you know what it'd be like in this house if you were filmed or photographed anywhere near the camp and your dad saw you. It'd be the end of your friendship with Asra.

I nodded. I know, Mum, but how about if I stop at that

bend in the lane and have a look, and if anything seems to be happening I forget it and come home?

She sighed again. All right, love. If you promise me you'll do that, you can go. Have you got your key, because I'll be at work when you get back. There's salad and pizza in the fridge.

Mum works at a charity shop in the village. I showed her my key and my mobile. I'll call you at the shop so you'll know I haven't been kidnapped or anything. Don't worry.

Mum snorted. Don't *worry*, she says. My daughter goes off to her quiet little village school, and the next thing I know I get a call to say somebody's blown the place up and my child's in hospital. *You*'d worry if you were a mum, Ruby Tanya.

I grinned. I think you'd worry as well – I *am* only twelve.

There's no need to be cheeky, young woman. I'll talk to you later.

Later, Mum. 'Bye.

I turned my collar up and set off towards school, squinting at the world through the rain-beads on my glasses, hoping I'd find everything just as usual at my best friend's so-called home.

- Seven
Ruby Tanya

I had no prob collecting my bike. There was a policewoman at the gate, who let me through when I explained. Stay away from the building, was all she said.

You know when you're getting near the camp, because of the sign. It's got rust spots, the words are faded and the whole thing's practically buried in long grass but there it is. RAF TIPTON LACEY 1/4 MILE, it says, in pink which used to be red. The bend is just after the sign.

Approaching it I dismounted, leaned the bike on the hedge, crabbed along the wet verge and peered through a tangle of hawthorn. A blue car was parked just this side of the gates and three men were standing in the road, hunched against the drizzle with their hands in their jacket pockets, gazing into the camp. I couldn't identify them, they were too far away, but I knew the car. It was Mr Holloway's Polo. Mr Holloway is the village barber. None of the men seemed to be carrying weapons, which was a relief, and there was nobody from TV or the papers.

17

Still, I didn't know what to do. There were no cameras, but my dad and Mr Holloway are in the quiz team down the Three Horseshoes. They play every Tuesday. If old Holloway saw me out here he'd be bound to mention it to Dad. I decided to wait a bit. After all, nothing much was happening: maybe those guys'd get fed up being rained on and go home.

I was getting pretty wet myself under the dripping hedge. Spider webs are pretty with rain-beads on them, but I wasn't sure where the spiders were and that was making me itch. I was glad when PC Willoughby's patrol car whooshed by and drew up behind the Polo.

PC Willoughby got out of the car and went over to the three men. Somebody inside the camp must have called 999. I couldn't hear what was being said, but after a couple of minutes and a few angry gestures towards the gates, the trio shuffled to the Polo and got in. The policeman stood watching as the barber started up, executed a three-point turn and accelerated in my direction. I turned my back as the car went by, so I didn't see who the passengers were.

The policeman was talking through the gates to some-body I couldn't see. I had to wait till he'd finished, which luckily wasn't long. Other vehicles were passing all the time, and I hoped nobody'd spot me who knew Dad. That's the trouble in a village: everybody knows everybody; you can't do anything on the quiet.

PC Willoughby didn't turn the patrol car round, but con-tinued towards Danmouth. When it was out of sight I emerged like a half-drowned hen from under the hedge, retrieved the bike and trudged along to the gate. Two men were opening them, but they saw me and reversed direction, swinging them shut with a crash. I was so startled I stood gawping through the bars with my mouth open. Four bearded men gazed back at me the way you might look at a venomous snake or a sabre-tooth cat.

- Eight
Asra

Where have you been? asks Father, as I slip into my seat at the breakfast table. You're quite wet.

I went for a walk, Father. The gates are closed. Three English men are outside.

Father nods. I know this, it is the trouble Mr Shofiq warned us of. You should stay away from the gates; all the children must stay away.

But what about Ruby Tanya, Father?

Your friend at school – *what* about her?

She will come, I think, like Saturday, but the gates will be closed.

Father shrugs. Then she will go home, Asra. He sighs. When I said *all* the children, I meant the English ones also. If there is fighting at the gates, it will be no place for children. Eat your breakfast, please.

No place for children. I stare into my porridge bowl without seeing it, my mind showing me video clips of my country in the days before we ran away. Mr Hussain next door, trying to fight the soldiers who have come to drag him off. His wife runs after them, then cries out and falls into the dust, where she lies blowing red bubbles at the sky, her mouth smashed by a rifle butt. Seven charred dolls I see one day, all that is left of a family, lying in front of their burnt-out home. Pretty little Sushi Bibi before she finds the cluster bomb, and after.

After is not so nice.

Father?

What is it, Asra?

Please, may I leave the breakfast?

Why, child, are you unwell?

No, Father, but I am seeing things, things that happened near our home. People . . .

I know. He nods, smiles a sad smile. I see those things too, so does your mother, so does everybody here. We must all try to push them away; they will grow dim with time. Drink your juice.

And Ruby Tanya . . . ?

Father smiles. While you are finishing your juice, I will walk down to the gates. If your friend is there I will give her your hello; if not I will leave your hello with the men on guard, who will give it to her if she comes later. How's that?

It seems sad to me, but I see it is the best that can be managed. Thank you, Father. I smile, and lift my glass.

- Nine
Ruby Tanya

I'm Ruby Tanya, I've come to call for my friend Asra.

One of the men shook his head. No children play today, they have teachings, prayers.

I nodded. I know about Fridays, but the children go to school Fridays, don't they? They'd be on their way now if there'd been no bomb.

The man shrugged. If there'd been no bomb; but there was. Things are not the same.

Me and Asra are the same. Best friends, always will be.

The man smiled briefly. Your father – he knows of this friendship?

Yes. Well . . . no. I mean, I haven't told him yet.

Why not?

Because he doesn't like . . . er . . . he thinks you and your people . . . oh, I dunno: he's *funny*, that's all.

Funny? The man shook his head. Your father is Ed Redwood, yes?

Yes, how d'you know?

He pulled a face. It is not a thing for children, Ruby Tanya. Go home, read a book.

It was raining harder. I could hardly see through my lenses and my hair was plastered to my skull. I was turning away when I spotted Asra's dad beyond the gate. I grabbed the top rail, stuck my face through the bars. Hello, Mr Saber, I've come to see if Asra's doing anything.

He walked across, shaking his head. I'm sorry, Ruby Tanya, Asra won't be leaving the camp today. She asked me to say hello. He looked me up and down. You're very wet. I should ask you in to sit by the stove, drink something hot, but . . . He indicated the four men.

It's OK, Mr Saber; I was just off anyway. Tell Asra, won't you? Say I'll come tomorrow, same time. 'Bye. I hadn't *meant* to be that abrupt. Five seconds and I was pedalling back along the lane with an aching lump in my throat, half-blind with tears. He called after me, something about tomorrow, but the wind through the hawthorns rattled a hard rain on my jacket and I couldn't make it out.

- Ten
Ruby Tanya

I went home. Well, what else was there to do in the pouring rain? I locked myself in and had a good cry. I'm not usually the weepy type: perhaps it was delayed reaction to yesterday. Anyway, I sat on the sofa and let it all out, and it made me feel better.

Actually I quite like having the place to myself. You know – watch whatever you want on the telly, play loud music, raid the biscuit tin; whatever. Nobody nagging, picking on you, telling you to tidy your room or come and peel these potatoes. I washed my face, called Mum and told her she could stop twitching, switched on the telly and vegged out, not really watching. The twelve o'clock news jerked me out of my trance: it was about our famous bomb again. I zapped it and went through to the kitchen.

I ate my pizza and chucked the salad in the bin, *under* something so Mum wouldn't see. A coffee and five Hobnobs did for pudding, then it was time for a poking-about expedition. Poking about means nosing where you wouldn't if your parents were in. Bedroom drawers are good: it's incredible what people keep in their bedroom drawers. The tops of wardrobes can also be worth investigating: I've found future birthday and Chrissy presents up there, and once there was this *amazing* video. I'm not going to tell you what it was like. I rewound it and whipped it off after a couple of minutes but it made me see Mum and Dad in a whole new way.

I didn't find any videos this time but I found something else, up in the office which is really an attic. The computer's up there, and a filing cabinet and loads of stuff to do with Dad's work as an estate agent. Dad doesn't like his stuff touched, so naturally I go through it pretty thoroughly on the odd occasions when I'm home alone. Mind you, I'm always careful to leave everything as I found it: like I said, he's a pain when he's upset.

I found this pamphlet, what they call a flyer. There wasn't just one; there were bundles of them stacked on the floor. I took one off the top and read it. This is what it said:

LAMP THE CAMP

An overwhelming majority of villagers are unhappy about the new role of the former RAF Tipton Lacey, now a dumping ground for illegal aliens. If you are one of us and have a vehicle, why not join us opposite the main gates at ten p.m. on Friday, 12 November for a non-violent direct action, the exact nature of which cannot be revealed in advance for security reasons.

DON'T SIT ON THE FENCE: YOU'RE EITHER FOR US OR AGAINST US.

At the bottom in small print it said, *Published and printed by*, with Dad's name and our address.

The flyer had been printed before the bomb, so naturally there was no mention. November the twelfth was a week from today. I had no idea what a non-violent direct action was, or that Dad was actually campaigning against the asylum seekers. If Asra's people were aware of his involvement it would explain how the men on guard knew his name, and why they'd slammed the gates in my face.

I folded my copy of the flyer and put it in my jeans pocket. I didn't know what I was going to do with it: show it to somebody perhaps, but who? And was there any point, when presumably it'd be all over the village by tomorrow?

I went downstairs, leaving no evidence of my visit to the office. I knew nobody was going to notice one flyer gone. I switched on the telly and sat gawping, while the wind racketed round the house and flung handfuls of rain at the windows.

- Eleven
Ruby Tanya

Dad put down his teacup and rubbed his hands together. Dark soon, he grinned. Time for big bangs.

It was bonfire night. Mum and I've never liked it much, partly because of Dad's love of bangers. I hoped he'd forgotten about it this year and I bet Mum did too, but no chance. He hadn't mentioned bonfire night, but he'd smuggled the usual box of fireworks home and hidden them in the shed, and I knew most of them would be bangers, the most powerful he could find.

So at half-six there we were, the three of us, in wellies, in the back garden. We never have a bonfire, which is just as well because it was chucking it down. *Does* it always rain on November the fifth, by the way, or is that an illusion? Dad was in charge of the fireworks, same as every year. He acts like he's the only one with enough brains to handle them properly. All the time he's setting them up and lighting them you get this running commentary, like he fancies himself as a bomb-disposal expert or something. The words plonker and sad spring to mind.

Some of the fireworks were quite nice, I suppose. A few. And of course there was the toffee. Plot toffee, Dad calls it. We have to have some, because he had it every bonfire night when he was a kid. In fact Mum uses his mum's recipe so it's exactly the same. I think Dad secretly wishes he could go back to being a boy: it's a wonder he hasn't preserved a pair of short trousers and one of those peaked schoolboy caps with a badge on the front, to wear on bonfire night.

Here's the weirdest bit though, same every year. He'll start off ultra-cautious, lighting the blue touch-paper at arm's length and standing well back, treating Mum and me to the commentary, talking about how stupid some people are with fireworks. Then, bit by bit as he gets excited, he'll forget his own advice and start doing daft stuff with bangers: holding them till they splutter, then chucking them over next-door's fence or rolling them under the shed, whooping like a loony as they explode. I'm always bursting to remind him what he's said earlier and I bet Mum is too, but we've never done it. He's such a baby it's not worth upsetting him. So we stood blinking and flinching, pretending to enjoy ourselves till he'd flung the final banger and punched the air one last time.

It was only half-seven when Mum and me kicked off our wellies, draped our sodden coats over chairbacks to dry out and collapsed on the sofa, relieved to have the ordeal over till next year. I was just getting comfy, gawping at a game show on the telly, when Dad came in the room. Here, Ruby Tanya, he said, nice little job for you. I twisted round to look. He'd got two great armfuls of Lamp the Camp flyers and a strip of sticky labels about a mile long. On every label, in big black capitals, were the words REMEMBER THE BOMB.

- Twelve
Ruby Tanya

I was smart enough to act like I'd never seen the flyer. I was like, *What* job, Dad? Where'd you get all this stuff?

He dumped the stacks on the carpet and the strip in my lap. All you've got to do, he said, is stick one of these in the top right-hand corner of each leaflet.

But there's hundreds, I protested. Thousands. It'll take me all night.

No it won't. If your mum and I help we'll have 'em done by bed time easy.

Mum peeled a flyer off the top, read it, looked at Dad. Lamp the Camp, she said. What does that mean, Ed? You're not thinking of setting the place on fire, I hope?

Don't talk daft, Sarah.

What does *lamp* mean, then?

Look. He pointed to a line and read it aloud: . . . *the exact nature of which cannot be revealed in advance for security reasons.* You know what that means, don't you? Means don't ask questions.

Mum shook her head. I'm not touching these till I know what they mean, Ed. I won't tell anybody else, but I have the right to know what I'm getting involved in.

You're not getting *involved*, Sarah, you're sticking a few self-adhesive labels on flyers. *I'm* the one who's getting involved. *Somebody* has to.

Why? asked Mum. Why not leave those poor people alone, Ed? They're not hurting anybody.

Aren't they? Dad was starting to get mad. What about this then, Sarah? He jabbed a finger at the labels: *remember the bomb*. If that's not hurting anybody, what is?

Yes, but you don't know who planted that bomb. Nobody does. You're just assuming—

Look, Sarah, the school's been there for what – a hundred years? Hundred and ten? And in all that time nobody's bombed it. These so-called asylum seekers arrive, and in less than three months the place is blown sky-high. Bit of a coincidence, isn't it?

Mum looked exasperated. Yes, that's exactly what it is, Ed: a bit of a coincidence. You might as well say the school's been there for a hundred and ten years, and the first time a prince visits the area it's blown up, so therefore the prince must've done it. It'd make as much sense.

He went ape-shape of course. Picked up the stacks of flyers and snatched the labels out of my lap. All right, he yelled, I'll do the job myself. Just don't expect any fireworks *next* year, that's all. I spend an hour in the pouring rain, not to mention the money, giving the two of you your own private display, and this is the thanks I get. Well that's it: *finito*.

He stormed out to the kitchen where he'd have the table to work on. We could hear him slamming stuff down, scraping a chair across the tiles, muttering to himself. Mum looked at me and I could tell we were thinking the same thing. No more fireworks, she murmured. If I'd known it was that easy, I'd have done it years ago. We both started giggling, quietly so he wouldn't hear.

- Thirteen
Asra

On Saturday comes a letter to Mr Shofiq. It is from Education Department. At ten o'clock everybody was in the social club where he read it two times: first in English, then in our language. It was about our school. The structural damage is less severe than the department feared, being mostly confined to one classroom. Though it will be some time before this classroom is back in use, the rest of the building has been inspected and declare safe, and after glazing work is complete, the school will reopen on Monday 15 November at the usual time of 08.30.

Everybody is happy: 15 November is nine days only. Flipping brilliant, Ruby Tanya would say. Or maybe not: English children like holidays better than school.

The drizzle was gone away but gates were shut again. I walked round the airfield. No planes come now; weeds are growing through cracks in the concrete of the perimeter track where I walk. I'm glad there are no planes: planes dropped bombs on my village four times; one bomb lay till

Sushi Bibi touch it, then *bang*, no more that funny little girl.

Out on the airfield is no people. I can go slow, I can think. Today I am thinking about school, because of the letter. In my village was a school. All the children attend. The teacher was Miss Aram, she was kind. Then one morning it was not Miss Aram, it was a man called Mr Younis. He was not kind. We said, Where is Miss Aram? He said, Gone. One boy ask where, and Mr Younis beat him with a stick. Then he made everybody change places, children of one language this side, children of other language that side. When we was all sitting like this he pointed to me and my friends. These children are goats, he said. They eat rubbish and pee on the ground. They stink. No decent child will talk to them, play with them, eat near them. They are goats.

We tried to keep going to school, but it was too hard. Mr Younis talked only to one side of the room. To our side he brought the stick: the stick was our teacher. We were beaten if we spoke our language, but if we answered in theirs he would shout, This language is for *people*, not goats, so we didn't know what to do. The other children wouldn't talk to us or play with us. Soon they learned that they could please Mr Younis by hitting us, spitting on our food, pretending to be sick if one of us came close. After school we were chased, tripped and punched and pelted with stones. We'd come home wounded and find our parents afraid to confront our tormentors, afraid to complain, because bad things were happening to them too. They knew the bad men wanted us driven out of school, not just in our village but all over the country, so after a few days we stopped going.

It wasn't holidays. Wasn't fun. We knew we'd grow up like goats, fit for nothing but to wander with our heads down, looking for what nobody else wanted and eating it. Our

33

parents knew this too; it was part of why they fled with us to England.

Anyway, that's why I was glad our school would open soon.

- Fourteen
Ruby Tanya

I woke on Saturday morning to a horrible suspicion. The more I thought about it, the more obvious it seemed. *Dad's going to make me deliver his flyers.* I even knew what he'd say: Your mother and I have to work, you're doing nothing special, the exercise'll do you good, blah, blah, blah. It was bound to happen. My only chance was to pretend to over-sleep, wiped out by the sheer exhilaration of his firework display. They'd been known to go out and leave me in bed so it just might work.

Breakfast seemed to last about a century, then Mum and Dad took it in turns to come upstairs and flush the loo. I lay on my side with the duvet up around my ears, absolutely still. Somebody – I think it was Mum – opened my door very quietly. I did this deep, rhythmic breathing till it clicked shut again. I even kept it up for a few seconds in case she'd got her ear to the door. In other words I was flipping brilliant.

After an age I heard the side door, then the Volvo. I gave

it five minutes in case they came back for something they'd forgotten, then got up and went down in my dressing gown. Even then I didn't relax: I wouldn't have put it past Dad to have left a stack of flyers and a note.

There was no stack, no note. I had six spoonfuls of sugar on my Cheerios and four in my hot choc, and I didn't brush my teeth. I put on designer jeans and my new top, the one Dad says makes me look like a trainee tart, and slapped on some of Mum's expensive make-up. I put my phone, key and dosh in the denim shoulder bag that matches my jeans, and set off to catch the Danmouth bus.

Danmouth's our nearest town. It's nothing to get hysterical about, but there's a mall with fashion shops and eateries and a Virgin Megastore. I phoned Millie Ross from the bus stop. Millie's my second best friend, after Asra. I'd have phoned Asra but she doesn't have a moby.

Hi, Millie, it's me. I'm at the bus stop. Fancy coming to town?

Uh ... I'll have to ask the crumblies, I'm supposed to go to the garden centre with them.

The *garden* centre? What for?

Choose bulbs for next spring. You know, hyacinths and that.

Oh, wow, I hope they give you a badge, Millie: I CHOSE BULBS AT THE DANMOUTH ROAD GARDENERS' WORLD, so every-body'll know how brave you've been.

I know, I know, but *you* know what parents're like. I'll call you back.

She got out of it, don't ask me how. I had to let the nine-o-five go by, but she was there in time for the nine thirty-five. We sat on the long back seat, hoping some lads would get on. Millie's parents and mine are completely different except in this one way: they *hate* us hanging out with lads. But with my folks working and hers choosing bulbs, I thought, there was no chance we'd bump into them today.

Shows how wrong you can be.

- Fifteen
Ruby Tanya

Sam Bradley and Jason Miller got on at the next stop. They're a year older than us and dead fit, especially Bradley. They said hi, but they sat near the front and when we stopped again two Year Eight girls joined them. We showed them we didn't give a stuff by gawping through the window.

There were yellow trucks in the schoolyard, and some guys in hard hats. Millie pulled a face. *They*'re not wasting any time, she growled, working weekends. No wonder the dump's reopening Monday week.

Monday *week*?

Oh yeah: didn't you get the letter?

What letter?

Millie shrugged. Letter this morning, from the Education Department.

Ah, I nodded. Mum and Dad left before I got up, they'll have seen it. I sighed. What a bummer. I hoped we'd be out till after Christmas, skip all that turkey and tinsel trash. The flipping *concert*.

Millie shook her head. You know how it is, R.T. Takes more than a bomb to put a dent in the season of goodwill.

At least it wasn't raining as we crossed from the bus station to the mall. We checked out Virgin and the clothes shops, then headed for Mocha Sins, which does speciality coffees at scary prices. My parents don't weigh me down with too much currency and Millie's about the same, so we got plain coffees and made them last, watching the world go by, and that's how I spotted Dad.

He was with two guys, one in a grey suit like his, the other in jeans and a donkey jacket. The suit could have been another estate agent, but Donkey Jacket looked like a soccer hooligan on steroids. I looked away as the three of them passed the plate-glass window we were sitting in. We weren't doing anything wrong – there wasn't a lad within spitting distance – but I didn't want to be seen.

Millie looked at me. What's up?

I pulled a face. Didn't you see my dad?

Your dad, where?

Just walked past with two other guys.

Well, so what? We aren't doing anything.

No, I know, but it's a bit weird. He's supposed to be at work.

Millie shrugged. He's an estate agent, showing two guys a property. What's weird about that?

I shook my head. Nothing. Where are they now?

Millie peered past my shoulder. If I'm looking at the right three, they're turning into Bessy's.

Dad's choice, I murmured. Bessy's is this deliberately old-fashioned teashop. The waitresses wear white caps and frilly pinnies and call the male customers sir, which is designed to attract slightly pervy men, if you ask me, but still . . .

When we'd nursed our coffees as long as we dared, we walked past Bessy's. I glanced in but they weren't in the window. If you wear a donkey jacket to Bessy's they don't give you a window table, they hide you. The thought of Dad having to sit in some shadowy corner not far from the toilets made me smile. If I'd known how my path and the hooligan's would cross in the near future I'd have smiled on the other side of my face, whatever that means.

- Sixteen
Ruby Tanya

I was dreading going home for lunch. Neither of my parents works Saturday afternoon and Mum brings fish and chips. It wasn't the fish and chips I dreaded, it was those flyers. They must be about somewhere, waiting for me to shove them through everybody's door.

Turned out I was wrong about that as well. We'd just sat down, and Dad was shaking vinegar over his chips like somebody putting a fire out when he looked across at Mum and said, By the way, Vikki took those leaflets round for me, didn't mind a bit. Nice change from sitting in the office, I suppose.

Mum speared a chip. Fine. Did *she* ask what Lamp the Camp means?

He shook his head. Certainly not. Vikki works for me, she minds her own business.

Good for her. I hope you're not starting trouble, Ed, that's all.

Dad shook his head. I'm not starting *anything*, love; those terrorists started it. I'm just helping the locals focus their anger.

You've *decided* they're terrorists, have you, the asylum seekers?

Of course they're terrorists. That's probably why their own country kicked 'em out.

It took me all my time to keep from yelling out, I was so mad. I wanted to say, Asra's not a terrorist, and neither are her mum and dad. I wanted to tell him that the guy in the donkey jacket looked more like a terrorist than anybody I'd seen at the camp, but I couldn't, could I? I kept my head down and tried to concentrate on my fish and chips, but it wasn't easy.

They fratched all through the meal. I'm glad Mum doesn't believe the same things Dad does, but I hate them fratching. As soon as we'd finished eating I escaped to my room. I sat on my bed, fished the crumpled flyer out of my pocket and smoothed it over my knee.

Lamp the Camp. Thanks to Vikki, this thing was all over Tipton Lacey. Was it true that an overwhelming majority of villagers were unhappy? I suppose it might be, especially after the bomb, but would *they* know what Lamp the Camp meant? Would loads of people actually drive out there next Friday night to take part in something *the exact nature of which cannot be revealed*? Sounds dodgy, right? Might even be illegal. A thought came to me: did Vikki shove one of these through PC Willoughby's door?

The more I thought about it, the less likely it seemed. *For security reasons.* That meant Dad was worried in case the wrong people got to know in advance about his plan. Of course, the wrong people might just be the asylum seekers, but if what he was planning was illegal it could also mean the police, in which case he'd have told Vikki to skip the Willoughby place.

You're going to think I'm awful, but I decided to push *my* flyer through the policeman's door. Nobody wants to be a traitor to their own dad, but if PC Willoughby stopped him from breaking the law I'd have done him a favour, wouldn't I? Saved him from jail, *and* saved Asra's people from whatever Lamp the Camp meant.

It's not as if I just rushed off and did it. I thought and thought about it, and it seemed right. In the end you can only do what you think is right.

- Seventeen
Asra

Walking back across the airfield, I remember the English men at the gate and I think, We will be goats here too, because of the bomb. When we go back to school in nine days everything will be different; nobody will play with us or speak to us. The teachers will be cruel. Perhaps we will be driven out of England, but where will we go? Even goats need somewhere to live.

And what about Ruby Tanya? Already her father doesn't like me, doesn't like any of our people. She's my one English friend; if she hates me now I don't think so I can stand it.

At lunch in the mess I can't stop thinking about this. At our table is twelve people, three families. They are Mr and Mrs Butt with the bully Shazad and his sister Saida, the Majid parents with their three children, and us. In our village, Butt and Majid families were not our friends and we are not friends now. Each father and mother whispers together so the others won't hear, and the children keep quiet. It is the same in the huts with their blanket walls.

Ruby Tanya is the only one I can talk to properly. If I lose her I might as well cut out my tongue.

I decide I must find her, not in nine days but now. I have to know if she is still my friend. Straight after lunch I walk again over the crumbling concrete of the perimeter track till I come to a place I've noticed on earlier walks: a spot where people have broken through the ancient fence and trampled flat the rusty wire in order to pick the mushrooms, which many are growing on the airfield at this time of year. There is a muddy track through the long grass, made by many feet.

By the gap in the fence I stop and look back. The huts are a long way off, I can only see their roofs and somebody's washing on a line, flapping. Children are playing in the grass but they are far away too, taking no notice of me. I step through the gap and into some bushes. I'll be in bad trouble tonight but I won't care, if my friend is still my friend.

- *Eighteen*
Ruby Tanya

PC Willoughby's house is on Aspen Arbour, in the new part of the village. It's a semi in a row of semis. Everybody calls it the police station but it's just a house with a blue porch light. It's a five-minute walk from Glebe Lane, where we live, so I wouldn't take the bike.

Mum and Dad were hating each other in separate rooms when I left, so nobody asked me where I was off to. It was a cool, cloudy afternoon, but dry. Mr Jarvis next door but one was putting his garden to bed for the winter, pruning back his fuchsia shrub. He looked up as I passed. Tell your dad I'll be there Friday, love, he wheezed. He's a good'un, your dad; deserves everybody's support.

Like a coward I nodded. I'll tell him, Mr Jarvis. I should have said, Tell him yourself, you horrible man, but you see, old Jarvis *isn't* a horrible man. Not usually. In fact there aren't many horrible people in Tipton Lacey at all. If they knew Asra, I bet Dad would be Lamping the Camp by himself on the twelfth. *Practically* by himself, anyway.

46

I soon reached Aspen Arbour. The Willoughby house is number four. I pulled the crumpled flyer out of my jacket pocket and stood looking through the hedge at the lounge window. I didn't particularly want PC Willoughby to know it was me pushing the thing through his door: I didn't want *anybody* to know. The patrol car was parked on the drive but nobody seemed to be moving in the lounge. With any luck I could tiptoe up to the door using the car as cover, shove the flyer through the slot and get away without being identified. I was about to set foot on the drive when I heard kids shouting and whooping. As I glanced towards the noise, a girl came pelting round the corner. Silky yellow trousers flapped round her ankles and a long scarf streamed out behind her. As she raced towards me I realized with a shock that it was Asra, with a bunch of lads hard on her heels, baying.

As I started towards her she looked up and saw me. Quick, Ruby Tanya, she gasped, the policeman.

I didn't tiptoe up that driveway, I sprinted. Instead of easing open the flap on the letter slot I started hammering on the door with both fists, yelling at the top of my voice. Glancing round I saw Asra make it to the gateway, but then the boys were on her, punching and pulling her down, shrieking, *Bomber, bomber, bomber*, mindless as they closed for the kill.

I don't *know* they'd have killed her – I doubt if *they* do – but as Asra fell the door flew open and I was sent reeling. PC Willoughby bounded towards the melee, roaring. A boy shrilled a warning and the gang scattered like minnows, leaving my friend in a spatter of blood on the path.

– Nineteen
Ruby Tanya

'S all right, love, you'll be all right. PC Willoughby squatted in his gateway, one hand cupping the back of Asra's head, the other holding a handkerchief he was using to dab at the cut on her cheek. He glanced up. Go get Mrs Willoughby. Ask her to bring the first-aid kit and a glass of water.

Between them the couple calmed my friend, cleaned her up, and having satisfied themselves she wasn't badly hurt, installed her on the sofa in their lounge with a cup of milky tea. I got tea too, and there was a plate of chocolate biscuits. Our police station's loads better than the ones you see on telly.

PC Willoughby leaned forward in his armchair. Now, Asra, he said gently, did you recognize any of those boys? Do you know their names?

Asra gazed at the policeman for a moment, then nodded. I see them all at school, but names... She hesitated, glanced at Mrs Willoughby in the other armchair, then at me beside her on the sofa, then at the hearthrug. My father says we must not bring trouble for ourselfs. If I say names there will be trouble, I think.

The policeman nodded. Trouble for those boys perhaps, but you see, Asra, if we don't do anything they'll think, Oh, right, we got away with that, let's do it again. I need to speak to their parents, that's all. He smiled. I recognized two or three or them myself, and I'd probably have placed the rest if they hadn't moved so quick. Nobody'll know you split on 'em, love, if that's what you're worried about.

So Asra gave him names, and I mentioned one or two myself. He wrote them down in his notebook, nodded and stood up. Right, girls, he said briskly, thank you very much. With a bit of luck we'll nip this spot of bother in the bud before it gets out of hand. We want no riots in Tipton Lacey, people taking the law into their own hands.

We were at the door when I remembered why I'd come to Aspen Arbour in the first place. I produced the flyer. These're round the village, I mumbled, thrusting it at him. I thought you should know. I didn't mention Dad, but of course I didn't need to, his name was on the thing.

Willoughby smoothed it out. Lamp the Camp, he growled. What the heck does that mean?

I shook my head. I don't know, Mr Willoughby. I looked at him. What you said to Asra, about nobody knowing . . .

He nodded. It's all right, love, no one'll know I got this from you. He smiled. You've done the right thing, Ruby Tanya, in case you were wondering.

I'd been wondering all right. I was still wondering when Asra and I turned the corner at the end of Aspen Arbour. The picture in my mind was of Dad being bundled into one of those black vans with POLICE on the side and shields above their windscreens. Make me *really* popular at home, that would.

Not.

49

– Twenty
Asra

I am walking in Beech Grove with my good friend Ruby
Tanya. On my face is a cut with a plaster, and a happy smile.
Those boys were hating me but Ruby Tanya is not. She
keeps looking at me as we go along. You OK? she is saying.
Yes, I tell her, I am *very* OK.

I wish we could go to my place, she says, but my dad . . .

I nod my head. I know; it doesn't matter.

I'm really sorry.

Don't be sorry. *I'm* not sorry. We are two friends still,
that's what matters.

Ruby Tanya smiles. Shall we check out Mayfields, then?
Mayfields is the village bread shop, but there are some
tables and they have coffee. It is handy if you can't be arsed
going into Danmouth. When she told me this Ruby Tanya
said, *arsed* is a bad word. Don't use it at home. This is how
she is difference from other kids; other kids teach us bad
words and don't tell us they are bad. They think it is very
funny if we say one to a teacher.

In Mayfields is not so busy, because Saturday afternoon everybody is shopping in Danmouth. We get coffee, sit down. How come you're out anyway? asks Ruby Tanya. Are the gates open?

I shake my head, tell her about the gap in the fence.

Won't you get into trouble though? she asks.

Yes, but I had to know if you still like me and you do, don't you?

Course I do, why shouldn't I?

There is the bomb.

So? She shrugs. Just because some turnip-heads decide to blame asylum seekers doesn't mean I've got to drop my best friend, does it?

I look to her over the rim of my cup. Your father . . . *he* blames us, I think.

Yeah, well he's one of the turnip-heads, Asra. We don't get to choose our parents, you know.

Yes, I know, Ruby Tanya, but families are important. I don't want you to get trouble with your family because of me.

I won't get trouble, she says. *They'll* get trouble, the turnip-heads. You heard what PC Willoughby said: he'll sort 'em out.

We talk and talk, happy to be together. I tell how the boys started chasing me, and how frightened I was till I remembered the police station. How surprise when I see she is there. Ruby Tanya tells me about the papers she found at home, the flyers, and all about her father and the fireworks. She is not glad our school will be mended in only one week and a half. I tell her I am very glad, but scared that everything might be different, kids hating us, teachers hating us too. I tell her about Miss Aram and Mr Younis. She says that sort of thing couldn't happen in England,

51

people wouldn't stand for it. I tell her I hope she is right.

It is a very good time at Mayfields till the man comes in. I do not know the big ugly person but Ruby Tanya does and she whispers a bad word. He is buying a pasty, staring at us as the lady wraps it and takes his money. When he has his change he comes across. You're Ed Redwood's girl, aren't you? he growls. Ruby Tanya nods and the man looks at me. Who's this then?

My name is—

I asked *her*, he snarls. Rude fellow.

Asra Saber, murmurs Ruby Tanya. My best friend.

Oh dear, says the man, shaking his bristly head. Oh dear, oh dear, oh dear. Take her home to tea, do you? Ruby Tanya says nothing and the man smiles a scary smile. No, I thought not. Daddy wouldn't be too keen, would he, budding bomber at his table? He laughs, turning away. I'll see you later, young Redwood. He shoots me a horrible look. I better not see *you* though, Miss Saber.

A very good time, broken now like Sushi Bibi's face.

- Twenty-one
Ruby Tanya

It was good seeing Asra, having a good natter. Shame about Donkey Jacket, the ignorant pig. He knew Dad, so my secret friendship would soon be up the spout. Never mind: they have to send us both to school, it's the law, so we'll see each other there if nowhere else.

We set off home at three because it gets dark so soon in November. We said ta-ta at the corner of Glebe Lane and I stood there for a bit, watching Asra walk off down Danmouth Road. We'd not arranged anything for tomorrow because we'd no idea what was going to happen. We might both be grounded for sneaking off. At the bend she turned and waved. I waved back, then sauntered on past the Jarvis place. He'd gone in, leaving the garden looking really neat.

As soon as I walked in the kitchen door I knew something had happened. Mum was at the sink, chopping carrots. Where've you *been*, love? she asked in an urgent whisper. Your dad wants to talk to you. I was in trouble and I knew it. *Wants to talk to you* is code for *feels like knocking you into the middle of next week.*

'S OK, Mum, I murmured, I was down Mayfields, that's all. I went through to the hallway and hung my jacket on the newel post at the foot of the stairs. Then I took a deep breath and walked into the lounge.

He was in his armchair opposite the telly, which he zapped as I walked in. If there was a button on the remote for zapping kids he'd have clicked me off too, I could tell. Sit down, he growled, indicating the other chair. What d'you know about *this*, Ruby Tanya? He flapped a crumpled flyer at me. I looked at it. It's one of your flyers, I said: the ones Vikki took round.

Not *this* one. He brandished the thing. This one's different, it hasn't got a sticker. What d'you say to that, eh?

Er . . . oh.

Is that all you can say, Ruby Tanya? *Oh?* D'you know who gave me this? Well, *do* you?

I didn't say anything – there was nothing I *could* say. I'd slipped up, made a boo-boo. I'd completely forgotten about the sticker, given PC Willoughby the only copy that didn't have one.

I'll *tell* you who gave it to me, shall I? He wasn't asking, of course; didn't give me time to reply but roared out the name. Frank Willoughby. PC Willoughby. And who gave it to *him*, eh? *You*, that's who. My own daughter, my flesh and blood.

Man, was he working himself into a state. Dad's never actually *hit* me, but I was beginning to think he might this time, and I reckon Mum thought so too because she stuck her head round the door. Ed . . . ?

Shut *up*, Sarah, he snarled. Get back in that kitchen and shut the door behind you. You probably think I'm kidding but I'm not: those were his exact words. *Get back in that*

54

kitchen. I was gob-smacked. I could hardly believe it. It was like one of those Victorian dramas on telly.

Mum couldn't believe it either. She stood in the doorway gawping at my dad, Tipton Lacey's answer to Soames Forsythe. Maybe that's what saved me from a battering, because I'm sure he was working up to something pretty drastic. Anyway, when Mum didn't move he seemed to realize he'd gone a bit over the top. He didn't apologize, that's not his style, but you could see by the way his fingers dug into the ends of the chair arms that he was struggling to get himself under control. He stared at the rug – he didn't know where else to look. When some of the redness had faded from his face, he mumbled about loyalty and blood being thicker than water, and sentenced me to no pocket money for two weeks.

I thought I'd got off light considering, but of course it wasn't over. PC Willoughby had done his worst but Dad's friend, the ugly one in the donkey jacket, hadn't.

Not yet.

- Twenty-two
Asra

It is a quarter to four when I creep through Mushroom Gap. This is how I am calling my hole in the fence: Mushroom Gap. It is coming dark but still I am hoping nobody has missed me.

It is no chance, as Ruby Tanya would say. Everybody is missing me. Everybody has been looking, even Shazad Butt. Father is very angry. Your mother, he says. Look at her, how red her eyes are. She thought you were dead. Cried and cried till I telephoned to the police, and the policeman told me boys have hurt you. See. He pulls me in front of a piece of mirror we have on the wall. Look at yourself. Bruises, grazes, a sticking plaster on your cheek. Do you think this is how your mother likes to see you? Is this why we brought you all the way to England, so that things can be for us like they were in our country?

I have never seen Father so angry. It frightens me more than those boys did, and when he starts to beat me it hurts more but I do not scream, because I know Shazad Butt listens through the blanket, listens for my screams. When he has done beating, Father flings me down and strides out, and I crawl to Mother and bury my face in her lap. She sings to me softly, stroking my hair so I will know she loves me. I weep and weep, but quietly, and deep inside me is a place where I cannot feel sorry that I went to Ruby Tanya.

- Twenty-three
Ruby Tanya

D'*you* get days when your mum and dad aren't talking? I bet you do, and isn't it a bummer? Especially when they communicate through you. You know – tell your father his dinner's on the table. Tell your mother your dad's not hungry. And so it goes on.

Well, I knew Sunday was going to be one of those days, so I called Millie Saturday night and arranged to meet her at ten next morning on the Green. It's not the world's most exciting venue, the Green at Tipton Lacey. It's got a duck-pond and some benches and an ancient horse-chestnut tree, and there's a post with a little red bin fastened to it where dog-walkers are supposed to dump the poo they scoop up. There was a brief craze last spring for grabbing kids' bags on the way home from school and emptying them into this bin, but it died out after two lads got suspended. Anyway, with Mayfields shut on Sundays the Green was where kids usually met, so straight after a grimly silent breakfast I set off, wearing a puffa jacket over my apprentice tart kit.

It was a typical November morning, damply grey with a raw, niggling wind – just what you don't need when you aim to stay out as long as possible – but at least it wasn't raining. Millie hadn't arrived when I got there so I waited under the tree. Its branches were bare, but the massive trunk sheltered me from the wind. Well, a bit.

What time d'you call this? I jeered, when she finally showed up. It was nearly a quarter past.

Sorry, R.T. Mum made me iron my school stuff.

What the heck for? There's no school till a week tomorrow.

I know. She's going through a *you're old enough to start looking after your own things* phase. You know what parents're like.

Tell me about it. Mine aren't talking. All you can do is make yourself scarce.

So what aren't they talking *about*, your folks?

Oh, it's some daft leaflet my dad's put out. Mum doesn't agree with it.

Lamp the Camp, you mean?

Yeah, how'd you know? Oh – you'll have got one through the door of course.

We did. My dad's taking the Shogun out there Friday. He reckons you dad's got the right idea.

I snorted. Tell him not to bother, Millie. Dad won't be there himself. Willoughby's given him the hard word.

He hasn't.

He has.

How'd *he* get wind of it – they never shoved a leaflet through *his* door surely?

No, I gave him one.

You? Split on your own dad?

59

Well yeah – he could've gone to jail, see? And then there's Asra, I didn't want anything happening to her.

Why, what *is* lamping? They're not planning to kill somebody, are they?

Don't ask me, Millie. Dad won't say what they're gonna do. Probably won't happen now anyway.

We stuck our hands in our pockets, trailed across to the pond and plonked down on a bench. Two Canadas waddled over hoping to be fed. Millie gazed at them. Christmas next month, she growled. I'd leave if I were you.

Whether it was sheer coincidence or something in Millie's tone I don't know, but the pair turned at once and after what has to be the shortest, most panicky take-off run ever witnessed, launched themselves into the air, gabbling like bingo let out.

Laugh? We nearly christened our jeans. Well – you *need* a laugh now and then, don't you? Specially on a miserable morning in November when you've no dosh in your pocket. Trouble with this laugh, it was cut short by a gruff voice saying, Morning, young Redwood. Dad home, is he?

I swiped a hand across my streaming eyes and looked up into Donkey Jacket's mocking face.

- Twenty-four
Ruby Tanya

Y-yes, he's home. Why?

The man shrugged. Bit of business, your dad and me. He glanced at Millie. Bomber not with you today then?

Bomber?

Kid you were with in Mayfields. Asian.

You mean Asra. Her dad doesn't let her leave the camp.

Good idea. There ought to be guard towers, electrified wire, keep 'em *all* in.

I should've told him it was thanks to turnip-heads like him my friend's parents daren't let her out. I felt like it, but I didn't. If he was off to see Dad I didn't want him saying I'd been rude. I stared at the grass and said nothing and he moved on.

Who's *that*? asked Millie, as soon as he was far enough away not to hear.

I shook my head. I dunno, someone Dad knows.

Didn't we see him in Danmouth mall yesterday, with your dad and another guy?

Yes, that's the first time I'd clapped eyes on him, or the other one. Looks a thug, doesn't he? Not the type I'd associate with my dad.

Millie shook her head. Can't go by appearances, R.T. That's probably a Versace donkey jacket he's wearing.

Yeah, right. You got any dosh?

A bit. Why?

I thought we might bus it into Danmouth.

What for? Nothing'll be open.

Something to do though, isn't it? Warm on the bus as well.

Millie shrugged. Can if you like, but what's wrong with *your* dosh?

I pulled a face. Condemned to grinding poverty, Mill. Two weeks, for grassing.

Serves you right, you moron. C'mon then.

We sauntered towards the shelter, which was occupied as usual by a knot of bored village dwellers, smoking and spitting. There are only two buses on a Sunday. It's a bit like living on Pluto.

- Twenty-five
Ruby Tanya

I phoned home from town, got Mum. Well, I couldn't face going home for lunch and they make such a fuss if I just don't turn up.

Danmouth six four six four seven eight, Sarah speaking.

Hi, Mum, it's me.

Where are you, Ruby Tanya?

Danmouth, with Millie. We're thinking of eating here so I won't be in for lunch.

How've you got to Danmouth? You've no money.

Millie paid for me on the bus.

And lunch – I suppose you're sponging on Millie for that too?

'Tisn't sponging, Mum; we're friends.

That's as maybe, young woman, but it isn't meant to work like this, you know.

What isn't?

Your father stopped your allowance as a punishment, Ruby Tanya. You're not supposed to dodge the consequences, carrying on as normal using other people's money. It's no punishment if you're not missing out on anything, is it?

Mum, do you think I *deserve* to be punished for what I did? I thought you were dead against this Lamp the Camp business, same as me.

That's beside the point, sweetheart. Your father has disciplined you. It would be wrong of me to support you in defying him.

I'm not defying Dad, Mum. I didn't *plan* to dodge the consequences – today just happened, that's all. Anyway, is it all right? *Can* I eat here? We'll be home before dark.

I suppose it's all right, since you're there and it's almost lunch time now, but . . .

What, Mum?

Well, sweetheart, there was a man here to see your father, and . . .

And *what*?

It seems he saw you yesterday with your friend Asra, and he mentioned it, and of course your dad was very cross. I don't mean to spoil your day, but I'm afraid you must expect more fireworks when you get home – metaphorically speaking, of course.

I know the guy, Mum. Donkey Jacket, I call him. But how does Dad know him?'

I've no idea, darling. Listen – have a lovely lunch, and try not to miss the bus home. If you do happen to miss it, phone me and I'll bring the car. *Don't* set off to walk home in the dark, d'you hear? And in the meantime I'll talk to your father, try to calm him down a bit.

OK, Mum, thanks. 'Bye.

I don't mean to spoil your day, but your father's oiling the thumbscrews and he's got the cat-o'-nine-tails in brine. So thanks, Mum. Thanks a bunch.

We ate at the Burger Bar, it's open seven days. When I told Millie what Mum said about me sponging she shook her head. You're not sponging, R.T. The day's bound to come when they stop *my* allowance for some imagined offence, then it'll be your turn to pick up the tab. She grinned. It's a sort of insurance: insurance against undeserved punishment, though I have to say yours is well deserved. Nobody likes a snitch.

What could I say? She was paying.

- Twenty-six
Ruby Tanya

He was lying in wait like a sabre-tooth flipping tiger. Before I even got the door closed he was like, And where have *you* been all day, young woman?

Danmouth, I said, peeling off my puffa to reveal the crop-top he loves so much. With Millie. Didn't Mum tell you?

Never you mind what Mum told me, you cheeky young devil. It's what a friend of mine told me that I'm concerned about. Who's Asra Saber?

Girl at school.

Best friend, according to *my* friend.

That's right, Dad, Asra's my best friend.

Comes from that camp, I suppose?

Yes, but she hasn't got a scruffy old donkey jacket and manners like a hyena.

He hit me then, an open-handed slap on my left cheek that shocked more than it hurt. He'd never hit me before. Never. Of course I shouldn't have said what I said, not to someone with Dad's temper. It was asking for it, but I'd thought it up on the bus, rehearsed it all the way home. I thought it was good, I suppose, too good to waste, and it had certainly proved effective.

How I managed not to cry I don't know, but I did. I covered the hot sting with my hand and stared at the floor, damming my tears. He didn't try to hit me again, but spoke in a quiet, husky voice. You're twelve, Ruby Tanya, he said. Twelve years of age: too young to criticize your parents' friends, or even to choose your own. Too young to go gallivanting round town half-dressed, and nowhere near mature enough to understand the ins and outs of what's being done to our country.

He paused, I suppose to gather his thoughts. I looked at Mum but she wouldn't meet my glance. The lump had gone from my throat. I knew I wouldn't cry. Shock had given way to something else. Hate? Well, hardly. He's got some dumb opinions but I know there's worse dads, much worse, so let's just say my stubbornness kicked in.

Dad continued. When school starts again a week tomorrow, you will stay well away from Asra Saber. You have a perfectly acceptable friend in Millie Ross, who I understand paid your bus fare today *and* bought you lunch. Now that's what I *call* a best friend. And in the meantime, you're not to leave the house for any reason. You can help your mother by cleaning up a bit, preparing vegetables, that sort of thing. In other words, young woman, you're grounded.

What a waste. What a boring, tragic waste of a week off school it is when you're confined to the house. Yes, I *know* it happens when you're sick, but when you're sick you don't feel like going out, doing things. And your folks don't make you chop veg either.

Worst thing was Friday. I'd planned to slip out Friday night, see for myself what Lamp the Camp meant, be there for Asra if she needed me. All through that useless week I kidded myself I'd still manage it somehow, but when the time came there was no chance. Dad made me stay in my room, and my room doesn't have a drainpipe outside the window or a cherry tree you can climb down like the rooms of grounded kids in adventure stories. In fact it's one of those windows that only opens a few centimetres, so you'd have to be a snake or something. Oh, and the stairs were a non starter because he spent the whole evening in the hall-way with his mobile. Thanks to my snitching, he hadn't dared be at the camp in person, but a bit of eavesdropping told me he was in touch with somebody up there. Knowing Dad, he'd probably given himself a fancy title: Co-ordinator sounds about right.

Anyway, it all meant I'd have to wait till Monday to find out what happened. From Asra, provided she made it to school. Provided she hadn't been hurt or anything. Provided Dad didn't handcuff himself to me and sit next to me in class all day to make sure I didn't talk to her.

Lend me your brain Dad, I want to build an idiot.

- Twenty-seven
Asra

It feels long, this week. At first I am happy, because I know Ruby Tanya is my friend. She will come to the gates same like before, to say hello. I am there Monday morning but she does not come. She does not come Tuesday as well. On Wednesday there is a little voice inside my head saying something is wrong, she is staying away, nothing will be the same. I am trying not to listen, telling to myself it is school next week, we will be together, but still I hear the little voice.

Thursday comes and I am wishing I had a mobile phone. I would ask Father but he has too much of worry. He has ask the people in London to please let him stay in England, Mother and me as well, but they do not reply. Father is a chemical engineer, he can do good work, but the papers are telling to their readers our people do not want to work, they want dole. This is not true, but we have no paper of our own so our voices are not heard.

Hate is a thing the eyes can't see, but it is gathering out-side the wire. Our men feel the press of it and talk of putting up fencing round the huts. I hope so they won't; walking on the airfield is keeping me from despair.

On Friday night comes a bad, scary thing. The men at the gates have seen many cars that evening, far more than usual. Some go by; some park at the roadside, facing the gates. The men are watching these cars, but nobody gets out and nothing happens. Then, at exactly ten o'clock, when our children are sleeping, the drivers of all the cars switch on their headlamps and press down on their horns. Our guards are blinded, they cannot hear each other for the din. They think the cars will crash the gates, that an attack is coming.

I am awakened by Father shaking me. 'Get up, Asra,' he says. Help your mother carry our things outside, these huts will burn. There is terrible noise, bright light through the window. Everybody is stumbling around, there are screams, babies howl as mothers and sisters snatch them from their cots and dash with them to the doors, blundering into dividing blankets in their panic, dragging them down. Mother thrusts a double armful of clothes and bedding into my arms and I run through the Butts' room, skittling their possessions. Outside it is brighter than day, dazzling head-lights everywhere I look. The din is deafening. They're on the airfield, cries a voice, we're surrounded. I dump my bundle on the grass, turn to go back for more, though the little voice inside my head is asking what good it will do. Mother approaches, a silhouette, limping behind a moun-tainous load. As I move to relieve her she trips over a stray toddler and sprawls in the mud.

They keep it up for thirty minutes, the racket and the glare. At precisely ten-thirty the noise ceases, headlamps dip and the villagers start up and drive slowly in convoy past the gate. What would have happened if they had attacked I cannot say, because they didn't. It emerges afterwards that they'd never intended to: Lamp the Camp was a protest, that's all; a demonstration, a sort of *son et lumière* show. A bit of fun, one man tells a reporter.

For us it is not fun. People who know guns and bombs do not laugh when awakened by noise and blinding light. It is too much like their dreams.

– Twenty-eight
Ruby Tanya

Idiot. You should've seen him Sunday morning, gloating over the paper. We made the nationals, he says, grinning all over his face. He held it up so Mum and I could read the headline: DEMO AFTER DARK – BOMB VILLAGE IN LIGHT AND SOUND PROTEST. It wasn't on the front page but there was a full column, with a picture in which perhaps a dozen cars could be half seen behind the glare of their own headlamps.

He read the whole thing out to us as we ate breakfast. Whoever had written it made it sound as though everybody in Tipton Lacey was there. Up to a hundred and fifty vehicles, was the reporter's estimate. He'd interviewed somebody called Sefton Feltwell, who had a mobile phone clamped to his ear and seemed to be directing the operation, which he said would last half an hour.

Who's Sefton Feltwell? frowned Mum, when Dad got to that bit. *He's* not from the village.

Sefton's London-based, said Dad. A contact alerted him to my plan and he offered to help.

Why? pressed Mum. Why would a Londoner interest himself in a little village protest, Ed?

Dad shook his head, impatient to read on. He's concerned about asylum seekers, Sarah, like thousands of other Brits. Doesn't matter *where* they are, city, town or village. Terrorists slip in with 'em, see? They look the same, the authorities can't tell the one from the other. That's why it's got to be stopped, now, before it's too late.

Neither of us interrupted as he read out the rest. To be perfectly honest I felt relieved. The piece made the whole thing sound harmless, if a bit silly. No stones, no petrol bombs or baseball bats; just half an hour of horns and headlights. It wouldn't have bothered Asra at all, something like that. She'd had worse in PC Willoughby's gateway.

So I was fairly happy that Sunday, even though it was back to school tomorrow. My grounding would end for one thing. I'd be out of the house and I'd be seeing Asra. Oh, I know I wasn't supposed to, but we were in the same class. Short of making me change schools there was no way Dad could keep us apart, and there's only one school in Tipton Lacey.

In fact, things weren't going to be quite as rosy the next day as I imagined. It's a good job we can't see the future, isn't it?

- Twenty-nine
Ruby Tanya

Keith Allardyce has one of those voices that goes right through you. It was the first thing I heard when I freewheeled into the yard that Monday morning. What you come back here for, eh? he was shouting. We don't want you in our school, stinking the place up, planting bombs.

He wasn't yelling at me, he was addressing a knot of camp kids who stood in a defensive huddle under the staffroom window. He had his gang with him, of course: a quartet of warped and witless hangers-on who, with their leader, had formed the nucleus of the gallant band which had fallen upon Asra two Saturdays ago. Now they stood in a semi-circle round the bully's victims, one of whom was Asra.

I'm no hero. When I challenged those five bog-dwelling failure-monkeys it wasn't because my best friend was in danger, it was because I'd spotted something they hadn't. Dimly, behind the net curtain that covered the staffroom window loomed the shape of Mick Traynor, our PE teacher and Tipton Lacey's answer to Arnold Schwarzenegger. He'd

74

not been there five seconds ago, and I knew he wouldn't hang around once he sussed what was happening here.

Hey, Allardyce, I yelled. why don't you stop pretending you're hard and go play with your Barbie doll, and take this bunch of bed-wetters with you?

It was all about timing. If Traynor let me down now, my end would be swift but messy. Luckily he didn't. In the time it took my message to locate Allardyce's brain, the big guy had crossed the staffroom and was pelting along the corridor to the lobby. By the time the bully's limbs got the instruction to propel their sad owner in my direction, Traynor was flinging open the door. As Allardyce lurched towards me he heard his name called.

ALLARDYCE, YOU NOXIOUS SPECIMEN OF FAECES!

The bully skidded to a halt. *Me*, sir?

I don't see any other specimen of faeces in the vicinity. Off somewhere, were you?

I – I thought I'd loosen up, sir, jog a bit.

Well don't let *me* stop you, lad. Ten times round the building before bell – GO!

It's not every day you get to watch an overweight bully lolloping round and round with his shoelace undone and his shirt-tail flapping. I for one made the most of it, but I think I knew even then I'd pay for it sooner or later.

- Thirty
Asra

She is brilliant, my friend Ruby Tanya. A hero. Keith Allardyce is a big bully and everybody is scared of him, but Ruby Tanya shouts at him to save my friends and me. If the teacher did not come I think so she will be hurt, but he comes to save us all. In England nobody is a goat, that's why we like to stay.

We watch Keith Allardyce jog till the bell, then it is assembly. Mr Ramsden stands on the platform looking serious. He is the head teacher, and this is what he is telling to us.

Today is a happy day for Tipton Lacey School, but it is a sad day too. Happy, because the builders have made our school safe again so that we can work, and also start to prepare for the Christmas celebrations. Sad, for three reasons. Firstly, and as you all know, the bomb which exploded in the shared area took the life of a fine young man, our student teacher Mr Conway. Mr Conway was only twenty, and though I know that won't seem particularly young to people your age, he was a man whose life had scarcely begun. Our second reason for sadness is that the same incident inflicted grievous harm on two of our Year Five pupils. Kelly Mountain and Andrew Farrell sustained ruptured eardrums, and this has left them profoundly deaf. I am told there is a surgical procedure involving implants, which sometimes enables patients like Kelly and Andrew to hear again, but it is a long, uncomfortable business, and I'm sorry to have to tell you that they are unlikely to be able to resume their schooling here.

As he is telling this to us, Mr Ramsden begins to cry. I never think to see a teacher cry, but his voice gets wavy and cheeks wet and he has to stop. Miss Hopkinson gives a tissue and whispers to him. In a minute he is all right, he says this.

Lastly, you should be sad about the recent behaviour of some of your fellow pupils. I am sad, because I have always believed that *all* of us here belong to the same family: the family of Tipton Lacey School. It doesn't matter who we are, or where we were before. The day we start to attend this school we become sisters and brothers, and we don't bully or pick on our sisters and brothers, *do* we, Keith Allardyce?

No, sir.

Do we, Craig Watling?

No, sir.

Do we, Jeannette Filmore, John Silverhill, Boris Barraclough?

No, sir.

He is a good man, but this assembly is scary for me. The names Mr Ramsden says are the names I tell to PC Willoughby. They will know, they will get me, like the children in my country, except I am not a goat here, I am *worse* than a goat. A goat smells bad but everybody knows it has no bomb.

- Thirty-one
Ruby Tanya

He's all right, old Ramsden. It *did* use to feel like a family in a way, with him as the dad, or maybe the grandad. Anyway, there was a good atmosphere and it was down to Ramsden; to his philosophy. There were people who didn't fit, of course; a few. Allardyce was always a bully, and when the camp kids arrived we got another in the shape of Shazad Butt, Asra's enemy. But even real families have their black sheep. Doesn't stop them being families.

Not the same now though. It was only Monday, school'd been going less than two hours but already I could feel the place had changed. There were actual changes, physical changes, but I don't mean them. I'm not talking about the workmen in the shared area, or the fresh paint on the class-room walls, or that those camp kids who're usually taught in the shared area because their English isn't so good were having to squeeze in with the rest of us for the time being. Maybe it was partly that somebody had *died* here, but there was definitely something else, and I got the feeling old

Ramsden was going to have his work cut out holding his family together.

I didn't have a chance to talk to Asra till morning break. When the bell went I got my jacket and hurried outside. She was waiting. We walked on the playing field. It was raining but we ignored it. I mentioned Lamp the Camp, expecting she'd dismiss it in a few words. I listened with dismay as she described the chaos, the fear. We thought they'd burn the huts, she said. We thought we were going to die. She told me something that had happened in her country, in the next village. The villagers were ordinary people, they'd done nothing wrong. One night, very late, they heard engines. Before they knew what was happening, trucks had surrounded the village, blinding everybody with their powerful lights. Men jumped out of the trucks and began running from house to house, shooting the occupants and burning their homes. They killed everybody, even babies. Two of Asra's aunties were among the dead. And it was the same on Friday night, she said. Engines, lights. We thought . . .

No, Asra, I cried, not in England. It was hard to speak through the ache in my throat. I suddenly saw they'd had no way of knowing, no way of knowing they weren't about to be butchered; that it couldn't happen here. A demo, a silly demo with a jokey title, had almost terrified the lives out of Asra's people, because my father had dreamed up Lamp the Camp knowing absolutely nothing about the world they'd come from.

I'll let him know, I promised myself. Minute I see him.

- *Thirty-two*
Ruby Tanya

There was a note from Mum on the kitchen table: *Dad and I are shopping for curtain material. Back around six-thirty. Will bring something for tea. Love, Mum.*

Curtain material. What brought *that* on all of a sudden? Nothing wrong with the curtains we've got. I'd psyched myself up to tell Dad how he'd scared Asra's people with his daft stunt, and now I'd an extra hour to wait.

I poked about upstairs but there was nothing new, except Dad had clipped the piece about Lamp the Camp out of the Sunday paper and filed it with the bomb coverage from the *Star* and a copy of his flyer. As usual I was careful to leave everything exactly as I'd found it.

I switched on the telly, watched an Aussie soap. They were having a barbie, which was just my luck because I was starving. I sat there slavering as a bronzed hunk loaded people's plates with steak and sausage. *Please, sir, I want some more.*

The news came on. I muted it and tried to follow what was

happening by reading the newsreader's lips. No chance – it beats me how anybody can do that. Without commentary, the stuff on the screen was pantomime, a succession of unconnected, meaningless images. I thought about Kelly Mountain and Andrew Farrell. Somebody had pressed the mute button on their world, reducing everything to this.

Then I saw a face I thought I recognized. There was some sort of march: people on the street behind the guy being interviewed, marching with placards. I pressed for sound but I'd missed the interview. The guy had turned away, was rejoining the march; ... *visible manifestation of growing public disquiet over the issue of asylum seekers*, intoned the reporter. He gave his name, said he was in London and returned me to the studio. A second or two later I remembered why that face was familiar. The guy was one of the pair I'd seen with Dad in Danmouth mall.

- Thirty-three
Ruby Tanya

I chickened out. Well, by the time they'd got out of their coats, unwrapped the boring-looking fabric they'd chosen and fussed about, holding it against the wallpaper, the carpet and the three-piece suite to see if it matched, the moment had passed. Also they'd brought fish and chips for tea because it was my favourite, and Mum made a point of telling me it was Dad's idea, so I'd have come across as ungrateful if I'd laid into him. Oh, I know there's never any shortage of excuses for taking the easy way out, but that's what happened and that's how I handled it.

I spent half the night thinking about the guy on the news, the one who knew Dad. I wished I'd caught the interview; wished I could stay up for the ten o'clock bulletin in case they showed it again. No chance, of course: nine's my bed time during the week.

Tuesday morning I waited till Dad roared off in the Volvo, then looked across the table.

Mum?

What is it, sweetheart? She was enjoying her second cup of coffee.

There was a guy on the news last night, leading some sort of march.

Oh yes, and what about him?

I recognized him. I've seen him in Danmouth with Dad.

She looked up. Well who is he, Ruby Tanya? What's his name?

I don't know, Mum.

Didn't it say, on the news?

I had the sound off.

Oh. Well, he's probably a client of your father's, looking to buy a property in the area.

But Mum, he was in London.

Yes, well, lots of people abandon London for some peaceful backwater, darling. She smiled brightly. Why didn't you mention it earlier, while your dad was here? He might have been interested.

I . . . dunno, Mum. I thought he might get mad, think I was spying on him that day in Danmouth.

Mum laughed. Honestly, sweetheart, you have the oddest notions. Why on earth should your dad think you were spying?

I shrugged. I don't know, Mum, but there was another man with them – the guy in the donkey jacket who called here a week last Sunday and blabbed to Dad about Asra.

Oh, *that* man. Mum frowned, shook her head. I didn't take to him at all. Cleaver's his name apparently, but your father didn't tell me anything else about him. You say he was with Dad and this other man?

Yes.

Well then, it'll be something to do with work. Mum smiled. I expect your father'll enlighten us when he's ready,

Ruby Tanya. Meanwhile, I think it's time you were off to school.

I read this in my magazine: *If you're worried about something, talk to your parents.* They should've added, *It'll get you absolutely nowhere.*

- Thirty-four
Asra

It is Tuesday, quarter past eight. Time to go to school. We are waiting in the minibus for Mr Malik, who drives us. Shazad Butt is not here, just his sister Saida. When I whisper to her, Is Shazad sick? she says, No, he will come with our father. I don't understand why Mr Butt will come to the minibus, and before I can ask he is here, with Shazad and Mr Malik.

Listen please, says Mr Malik. Mr Butt has something to say to you all. We look to Shazad's father, who has climbed into the bus, bent over so his head won't hit the top. He begins.

Children, he says, my son has spoken to me about yesterday at school, how some of you were frightened and bullied in the yard. He lays his hand on Shazad's shoulder and I know from his face Shazad is feeling very important. I think to myself, you are a bully too, but I do not say this. Mr Butt continues.

We know about bullies. We are here in England because

of bullies. Bullies drove us from our own land. He sighs, shakes his head. We cannot let ourselves be driven out again, there is nowhere to go. So. He looks at us all. It is necessary that we defend ourselves before the bullying goes too far. We don't want trouble, at school or anywhere else, but we are entitled to defend ourselves, so this is what we will do. At morning break each day, and at lunch time and afternoon break, my son and some of the older boys will form themselves into a squad to protect the smaller boys and the girls. You will help with this plan by staying always together in the yard, so that the boys can watch over you. They must never start trouble, but they will defend you if you are threatened.

Mr Butt makes me sad with his words. Sad and frightened. School has been a good place, a place where we could feel safe. These words – *squad, defend, protect* – they are words I remember from my country; they go with guns and bombs and blood, not with school.

Not with the one big family.

- Thirty-five
Ruby Tanya

Something bad happened Tuesday lunch time. I mean, really bad. Somebody jumped a Year Five kid and gave him such a kicking that Miss Hopkinson had to call an ambulance.

It wasn't in the yard. Wouldn't have happened there because some of the biggest lads from the camp have got themselves together into a sort of posse to guard the girls and smaller boys, so it happened in the boys' cloakroom.

The kid was badly hurt, but not to where he couldn't talk. Miss Hopkinson put him on the camp bed they keep in the first-aid room for fainters and so on, and old Ramsden comes and questions him. He's like, Who was it, Asif? Who did this to you?

Sir, I don't know, says Asif.

You don't *know*? goes Ramsden. Somebody wrestles you to the floor and proceeds to kick you repeatedly in the back and stomach and you don't recognize him? I can't see how that's possible, Asif.

No, sir.

Was he a Year Six perhaps, or Seven?

Sir, I don't know.

What about his hair? Was it blond or dark? Did he wear it short or long?

Yes, sir, it was blond or dark, short or long.

He was more scared of his attacker than he was of the head, and you can't blame him. Whoever did it probably promised more of the same if he dobbed him in. *I* know who it was, and I bet Ramsden has a fair idea as well. Neither of us can prove it, but Keith Allardyce, who'd been sullen following his unsponsored jog with Traynor, swaggered round the place all afternoon looking like the cat that got the cream. You work it out.

The infirmary phoned Ramsden and he sent a note round. We were having maths with Boyd, who read out the note. The kid had two cracked ribs and bruising. They were keeping him in overnight for observation, but there was no cause for alarm. The boy's parents were at his bedside. At the end of the note Ramsden had put: *If Asif's assailant will own up before the end of the school day, I will do my utmost to treat it as an internal matter, rather than involving the police.*

As if, Asif.

– Thirty-six
Asra

I am about to get in the bus when Ruby Tanya calls my name. I'm sorry, she says, about Asif.

I look to her. You did not beat Asif, I tell her. You must not be sorry to me.

No, she says, of course I didn't do it. I meant I'm sorry it happened. Are we still friends?

Oh yes, I tell her. Much is difference now because of the bomb, but not with you and me. I will always be your friend.

Triffic, smiles Ruby Tanya. Listen – you'll have to get a moby so we can talk.

I nod. I know, I will speak to my father, but . . .

Not easy, with everything that's going on. I understand, honest. See you tomorrow?

Yes, tomorrow.

As the bus is starting to go, somebody behind grabs both of my plaits and pulls my head back till I am seeing this angry face. It is Shazad Butt. What did she want? he says.

Who? You are hurting my head, Shazad.

You know who. He tugs harder, water comes to my eyes.

She was saying sorry about Asif.

Ha! Shazad squeezes my hair. She is not sorry, she is glad. They are all glad.

Not Ruby Tanya. She's my friend.

He squeezes till I cry out. He brings his face very close and hisses, She is not your friend, Asra, she is English.

You want to be English, I tell him. Your father wants to be English.

That is difference, he snaps. We want to be English, but not like them. They are cruel.

You are cruel, I cry. It is you hurting my head, not English. Let me go, Shazad.

He lets go my plaits, but only because Mr Malik has heard my cry and is looking at him through his mirror. Shazad sinks into the seat behind mine, talking softly so Mr Malik won't hear. Mr Ramsden says we are one family but we are two: the English family, and our family. You must decide which family is yours, Asra Saber. Nobody can be in two families.

Without turning round I say to him, Two families can be friends. We have seen in our country what happens when they are not. We must be friends, or we will do terrible things to each other. If we do terrible things, England will be same like our country: some people will be the people, others will be the goats. *We* will be the goats.

Ha! goes Shazad, but then he is quiet. I mop my eyes with a tissue and look out of the window at pretty little Tipton Lacey, which tanks and planes would ruin in an hour.

– Thirty-seven
Ruby Tanya

I'd reached the corner of Danmouth Road and Glebe Lane when the patrol car drew up beside me and PC Willoughby stuck his head out.

Ruby Tanya?

Yes.

I wanted to thank you for alerting me to that demonstration Friday night. Could have turned nasty if it hadn't been for you.

I looked at him. It *was* nasty, I said. The people were scared witless. I've been wondering why you didn't stop it.

He pulled a face. I couldn't *stop* it, love – it wasn't clear any laws were being broken. But I was on hand to keep the lunatic element from taking things too far.

Lunatic element?

He nodded. Young lads with baseball bats, drunk, spoiling for a fight, crammed into a couple of old bangers. No knowing what they might have done if I hadn't been there.

Oh, I didn't know about that, Mr Willoughby –

paper didn't mention it. Could have been worse, then?

Much worse, Ruby Tanya. He smiled. Well, better get on. Thanks again.

Wait! The window stopped halfway up, came down again.

What is it, love?

There was a guy there Friday night, Sefton Feltwell, a reporter interviewed him. D'you know him?

The policeman nodded. Know *of* him, yes. Why?

Who is he? My dad seems to know him, says he's from London.

Yes, that's right. Feltwell lives in London and he's a nasty piece of work; secretary of a fringe political party called Britain First. Nazis. Tell your dad to steer well clear of that feller, Ruby Tanya. He's trouble.

Tell my dad? *Tell* him. I laughed. You don't know my dad, Mr Willoughby. He'd rip my head off and pour boiling oil down the inside of my neck. He's not the sort of guy you *tell*. A thought struck me. This Feltwell, does he have a friend? Big, brutal-looking guy in a donkey jacket, name of Cleaver?

The policeman nodded. Martin Cleaver, known to his friends as Cave-Troll Cleaver. Feltwell has brains but no muscle, Cleaver's the opposite. He's the party's chief heavy. Don't tell me your dad knows *him* as well?

I nodded. I . . . think he might.

Oh dear. He shook his head. Attracted to Tipton Lacey by our spot of bother, I shouldn't wonder. They like that sort of thing. Well. He twisted the key in the ignition, looked up at me. You might just drop a hint at home, love – say I'm aware these fellers're around and I've got my eye on 'em. See you.

The car rolled forward, the window slid up. Just before it closed completely he called something I didn't quite catch, but it sounded like *dangerous people*.

- Thirty-eight
Ruby Tanya

I didn't mean to say anything about Dad's dangerous friends. Not to him, not to Mum. They were just about speaking to each other and I didn't feel like stirring it up again.

Good day, sweetheart? goes Mum as I walk through the door. She was defrosting something in the microwave.

I pulled a face. Did *you* ever have a good day at school, Mum?

She smiled. Looking back, it seems I had lots of good days. Perhaps they didn't strike me as particularly good at the time, though.

I went through to the hallway, hung my bag and jacket on the newel post. It was ten to four; Dad wouldn't be in for another hour and a half. I returned to the kitchen.

Keith Allardyce beat up Asif Akhtar today, I said. Put him in hospital.

Oh dear, gasped Mum, how awful. The microwave pinged, she opened the door and took out some pieces of breaded fish. We hadn't *that* sort of thing to cope with in my day, certainly. Is Asif badly hurt?

I don't think so. Cracked ribs, bruises.

Still, that's bad enough. What happened to Keith Allardyce?

Nothing.

Nothing?

No, Akhtar was too scared to dob him in, so Ramsden couldn't prove it was him.

Young thug. Mum shook her head. I hope this isn't the start of some sort of racial conflict at school, Ruby Tanya. There's enough of that everywhere else. She dropped potatoes into the washing-up bowl, turned on the cold tap. Have you got homework?

Yes, Mum – English and Maths.

Why not do it before tea, dear, get it out of the way?

Well, why not? I snagged my bag off the post, bounded upstairs and shut myself in my room. English is dead easy but maths is a pain. With Millie it's the other way round, so I got her on the phone and we helped each other. It's not cheating, it's co-operation. We'd only just hung up when my moby beeped. I couldn't think who it could be.

Hello?

Is this Ruby Tanya, please?

Asra?

Yes, it is me.

Where are you – the social club?

No, I'm in the hut, lending Father's mobile.

Brilliant! So what's happening out there?

Nothing is happening, Ruby Tanya. I just wanted to call.

Glad you did. Done your homework?

Yes, or I would not be having Father's phone. Listen.

She told me about Shazad Butt, what he said on the bus.

She practically had to whisper because there was only a blanket between her and the bully. What a way to live.

He's a plonker, I told her when she'd finished. A sad, twisted plonker, so listen: don't chuck out of the family, Asra. The *one* family. I asked PC Willoughby about that horrible guy we met in Mayfields. He's called Cave-Troll Cleaver and he's trying to stir up trouble in the village, him and some others. I think they want to split everybody up, make us hate each other. We mustn't let them do that, Asra.

I know, it is what happened in my country. I told you, remember? We became goats.

Oh yeah, I remember now.

Anyway, here's my father. We will talk tomorrow, Ruby Tanya. Goodbye.

'Bye, Asra.

Got to stick by one another. *Got* to. It isn't cheating, it's co-operation.

- Thirty-nine

Asra

We are eating breakfast when police come. This is not PC Willoughby; there are no chocolate biscuits. Four men with shiny helmets and guns, jogging across the mess to our table. They are looking at my father. One says, Gulbankar Saber?

I am he, says Father. He is looking startled, a little afraid.

We'd like you to come with us, Mr Saber.

Where? What is the matter?

There are questions we'd like to ask you, down at the station.

Questions? Can you not ask them now please, here?

I'm afraid not, sir. If you refuse to co-operate, we have the authority to—

I am not refusing, sighs Father. He scrapes back his chair, stands up. Mother is clinging to his hand, starting to cry. The Butts and Majids sit silently watching. Two police take Father's arms, begin to lead him away. Mother lets go his hand with a little scream. Father twists round to look at her. Don't worry, Nusrat, he says. It is a mistake; everything will be all right.

My mother gets up to follow, but Mr Majid holds to her arm and says no. I am glad, because I am remembering Mr Hussain's wife in our village, clubbed in the mouth till she lies in the dust, blowing red bubbles at the sky.

I do not know till after what happens to Father. It is a long, terrible day for me at school. I walk with Ruby Tanya on the field. She listens as I talk, lends me a tissue when I cry. Nobody comes to tell me I am choosing wrong family, even Shazad. In English I cannot stop weeping. I have to tell Mrs Rule the police have taken my father. She pats my shoulder, tells me she's sure everything will be fine, sends me out to sit by the cloakroom door till I feel better. She does not understand but she is a good woman. She even lets Ruby Tanya keep me company.

It seems to never end, this Wednesday, but it does at last and I am on the bus, riding home, scared what might be waiting for me there. All of the children are quiet, even Shazad. When someone is in trouble it frightens all of us. We want so much to stay.

When I come through the blanket there is Father, holding Mother's hand. I run to him, hug his neck. He was right, I laugh to myself, it *was* a mistake, but I am wrong. Later, in the mess, I listen as he talks to Mr Butt and Mr Majid. He is angry.

They're investigating the bomb, he tells them. All of us are suspects – they must have gone through everybody's papers. When they found out that I'm a chemical engineer, they thought they had their man. Grilled me for hours. Where did I qualify? What sorts of projects did I work on in my country? Had I worked with any chemical substances since I arrived in England? They were taping everything. I asked, Should I have a lawyer? and they said, Why do you need a lawyer if you've done nothing wrong? They took my jacket, scrapings from under my fingernails, hairs from my head. When they finally let me go and I got back here, Nusrat told me men had searched our room; thrown everything around, broken some items, taken others away. Father sighs, shakes his head. They had to let me go, but all of this will not help me get permission to settle here in England. There's probably a rubber stamp on my papers: SUSPECTED TERRORIST.

So, we are happy Father comes back to us, but underneath, not happy. I would like more talk with Ruby Tanya, but I dare not ask Father tonight. He probably thinks police is tapping to his phone, and who knows? Maybe he is right. Do such things happen in England?

- Forty
Ruby Tanya

I tried to keep it friendly when Dad got in and the three of us sat down to eat. I wasn't going to mention Asif, PC Willoughby or my conversation with Asra, but it was warfare anyway. As soon as Mum put Dad's plate in front of him he poked the haddock fillet with his fork.

Cardboard, he says. If you must give us fish, Sarah, you might at least buy it fresh and cook it yourself instead of taking the lazy way out.

Mum's face went from November pale to incandescent as the pressure rose inside her head. I ducked and concentrated on my food.

Ed – she started quietly, the volume mounting as she eased open the valve of her anger – I worked six hours today in the shop. It was busy, and when we closed I had less than two hours in which to shop, get home, change, peel potatoes, top and tail runner beans, make parsley sauce, lay the table and put a hot meal on it. All you had to do at the end of *your* so-called working day, during which no doubt the famous Vikki did most of the actual work, was to sit back and wallow in the warmth of your own importance as the Volvo whisked you home.

Oh, she's good when she really gets it on. I bet they heard that *warmth of your own importance* in Danmouth. Dad muttered and mumbled and nudged his fish round the plate. *I* work, he said. I know more about work than you'll ever know. Five clients I chauffeured round today: *five*, and every one of them an awkward so-and-so. You've no idea.

Was one of them Cave-Troll Cleaver? I asked. I didn't mean to, I'd wanted to stay out of it, but it slipped out and now it was too late.

Dad's head jerked up. How d'you know that name? he glowered.

He came here, I murmured. You introduced him to Mum.

Yes, as Mister Cleaver. *Mister* Cleaver. Where'd you get Cave-Troll, Ruby Tanya?

PC Willoughby.

PC Willoughby ought to be out catching burglars instead of swapping gossip with schoolkids. What was he saying about Mr Cleaver?

I pulled a face. I asked about that other guy first – Sefton Feltwell – because I saw him on the news leading some sort of march in London. He says Feltwell's boss of something called Britain First.

Dad nodded. That's right. And how'd you get round to Mr Cleaver?

I asked PC Willoughby if he knew someone called Cleaver, because me and Millie saw him and Feltwell with you at Danmouth mall.

Did you? And what did PC Willoughby say to that?

Oh . . . he said Mr Cleaver was known as Cave-Troll but

101

he didn't tell me why. He said *he's* part of Britain First as well.

Mum, who'd sat listening to this while she cooled down, broke in. Let me get this straight, Ed. The chap who came from London for your demo, Sefton Feltwell, heads up a political party?

Yes, he does.

Nazis?

Some people call them that. Wimps.

And Cleaver's well up in the party too?

'Sright.

And you're involved with them in some way?

I am. They're impressed with me, and they've got plans. Big plans. Lamp the Camp was just the start. You wait. It won't be long before you're seeing *me* on the telly, *me* in the papers. And there'll be money too, if everything goes according to plan. Money, power, and not an asylum seeker in sight. *That's* the future we're looking at, Sarah.

PC Willoughby reckons they're dangerous people, I murmured.

No, Ruby Tanya, snapped Dad. He's got it all wrong. The dangerous people are up at that camp, but they won't be there much longer. It's a valuable stretch of real estate: too good to waste on terrorists. Just you wait and see.

- Forty-one
Ruby Tanya

First thing Thursday morning the whole school assembled in the hall. The head teacher had something to say to us. I thought it was bound to be about Asif Akhtar; everybody assumed that, but we were wrong. It was about Mr Conway, the student teacher killed by the bomb.

Some days ago, said Ramsden, the police were in touch with me about something their forensic people had discovered during the course of their investigation. It seems our Mr Conway was a finer man even than we imagined, because it turns out he didn't just happen to be standing near the device when it exploded: he'd found it and was attempting to carry it outside.

Ramsden had to break off as assorted gasps and murmurs arose from the assembly. I don't know what was going through everybody else's mind, but I was trying to imagine what'd happen to you if you were holding a bomb and it went off. Would you see the flash, know you were a dead man a split second before everything went black?

When the hubbub faded, Ramsden continued. Think what that means, girls and boys. It means Mr Conway spotted the bomb and recognized it for what it was, but he didn't react the way most people would. He didn't start running or throw himself down behind a desk or table in a desperate attempt to save himself. In those last, precious moments of his life, our Mr Conway wasn't thinking about himself at all: he was thinking about Tipton Lacey Middle School. He was thinking about *us*.

Old Ramsden spoke these last words very softly, and you could hear one or two people sobbing. He waited a bit with his hands crossed in front and his head bowed, like somebody at a graveside. There were sniffles; tissues were plied and put away. It was quiet.

Heroism of that order deserves to be marked, he went on. It deserves never to be forgotten, and it won't be. I have spoken with Stuart's parents, and with the Education Department, and having obtained their agreement I can inform you that when the restoration work is complete and the shared area reopens, it will be known as the Stuart Conway area, and a portrait of Stuart will be on permanent display there.

Murmurs, sniffles and a low *hear hear* from Mr Traynor. Ramsden turned and left the platform holding his handkerchief to his face as the rest of us trooped to our classrooms. The assembly had been an emotional experience for us all, and I for one would recall it with very different feelings in due course, when subsequent events had cast it in a new, less inspirational light.

- Forty-two
Asra

I am happy when Mr Ramsden tells to us about Mr Conway. Not happy because he is dead, happy because it is good his name is remember. My friends are happy too. We feel hope that our school will be a place of peace.

It is soon destroyed, this hope. After morning break it is PE with Mr Traynor. He likes for us to have PE outside in the fresh air, but today it is drizzle so we are having it indoors. We will begin with a warm-up, which is jogging clockwise round the hall. Ready, says Mr Traynor, *Begin*.

We have jogged only a few steps when screaming starts. I look where it is and see Keith Allardyce, hobbling and howling. He is a very silly boy and everybody thinks he is having a joke, even Mr Traynor. Allardyce, he barks, stop mucking about or I'll tear your arm off and beat you to death with the soggy end. Mr Traynor wouldn't do anything like that of course – he says things to make us laugh – but Keith Allardyce isn't laughing. He has fallen on the floor, tearing at the laces of his trainers. He is crying very much.

Mr Traynor sees the bully is not having a joke and runs to him. Keith is shouting, *My shoes: there's something in my shoes*. Mr Traynor squats, tells him to keep still and starts untying a trainer. When he eases it off his foot the boy screams very loud, and when he holds it upside down to look inside, blood splashes on the floor.

I don't see anything else because Mr Traynor tells us to get dressed, go back to the classroom and read our library books, except Tasmin Unwin who has to run and fetch Miss Hopkinson.

Keith Allardyce doesn't come back. Mr Traynor does, but he won't tell us anything. We read till lunch but not really; we are pretending. After we eat we don't go out like everybody else, we line up in the hall and Mr Ramsden comes. Then we find out.

In the craft area are modelling knives with very sharp blades, like razors. These blades come out so you can put in new ones. Somebody has stolen six new blades and pushed them up through the soles of Keith Allardyce's trainers, three for each foot. They don't pierce the inner soles till Keith starts to jog, then they are driven deep into his feet. Trembling with anger, Mr Ramsden tells us that when he finds out who did this, that boy will be expelled and given to the police.

When he is saying this, Mr Ramsden is looking at our boys, the boys of the camp, and I know why. Like me he thinks this was done because of Asif Akhtar: it is revenge. I am watching Shazad Butt with the corner of my eye. When the head says *given to the police*, Shazad swallows hard and I know it was him. I do not like Shazad and it is an awful thing he has done, but still I feel sorry for him. If he is found out, expelled from school and charged by the police, his whole family may be deported. In our country are men waiting to kill them. He must be terrified.

He gives no further sign though. Mr Ramsden paces up and down in front of us for half an hour, firing questions. We are all very frightened; he could accuse any one of us, even a girl. We are glad when the buzzer goes and he sends us to registration. I'll find you, he says before we go. *Somebody* must have seen you entering or leaving the craft area. I'll find that eyewitness, and then I'll find you.

It is gone, our place of peace.

- Forty-three
Ruby Tanya

Friday it was all in the *Star*: Asif's beating, Keith's feet, the plan to rename the shared area for Stuart Conway. Mr Ramsden had hoped to keep the nasty stuff out of the press, but both sets of parents had gone public about what had been done to their sons. Asif's dad told a reporter he thought the teachers at Tipton Lacey School were prejudiced against asylum seekers' children, while Allardyce senior accused them of favouring the refugees over the village children. There was a nice piece about the shared area, but it was spoilt by the other stuff.

Dad loved it though. He brandished the paper at Mum and me across the table. See what happens when you wash your coloureds with your whites, he crowed. Daft pillock.

Mum looked at him. You're not exactly helping, are you, Ed? Stirring the villagers up, attracting trouble-makers from London.

Dad heaved an exasperated sigh. What I'm doing, Sarah, is trying to preserve the English way of life. We've got a lovely little country here, and some of us want to keep it that way.

Mum nodded. And some of you think this is a good way of doing it, eh? Frightening people, turning them against one another?

Dad scowled. For goodness sake look back at history, Sarah. When this country was great, right, when Britannia ruled the waves, there were none of these asylum seekers or refugees or whatever you want to call 'em dossing around, making the place look untidy. Britain belonged to the British; everybody knew where they stood. A foreigner was *Johnnie foreigner*. There was none of this political correctness forcing you to call him something else.

History, said Mum. All right – why d'you think people choose Britain, Ed? When they need a refuge, I mean.

That's obvious, Sarah. They come for the benefits, don't they? The dole, NHS, all the other stuff we chuck at 'em for free.

Mum shook her head. Before all that. Hundreds of years ago. Why here?

It didn't *happen* hundreds of years ago. Like I said, Britain belonged to the British.

Oh, so what about the Huguenots, the Flemings, the Irish, the German Jews, the Poles, the Hungarians, the Greek Cypriots, the Ugandan Asians? Why did they all choose *our* country, Ed? Which of them started the rot? Exactly when did we start going to the dogs?

Ha! went Dad. That's your hippy mother talking, Sarah. You don't know what you're on about.

Yes I do. All those people *are* Britain, Ed. They're us. We're a queer mix, we British. All sorts of blood in our veins. Maybe that's why our country's been a byword for fairness, for tolerance. A byword for *freedom*. We've taken them in, treated them like parts of ourselves and life's gone on. If we close our borders, start turning frightened people away, we throw away the very thing our country is respected for. It's you and your lot, not the asylum seekers, who are soiling Britain's reputation. There was a song, Ed, during the Second World War: *You Can't Do That There Here*. It meant we'd have no Nazis, no Nazi ways in Britain. It *defines* our country, that song. It should be the national anthem.

I wish you could've seen Dad's face when Mum laid into him like that: it was better than *Lord of the Rings*.

– Forty-four
Asra

My parents take the Tipton Lacey *Star*, so do other families at the camp. Those who read English tell the news to those who don't. Most weeks it is nice news, like a wedding or a flower show. It is a way to practise the language, and also to learn about this pretty village we have come to.

This week is too much nasty news. Asif Akhtar is in it, and Keith Allardyce. Parents have said bad things and the paper has printed them. Nobody wants to read these things aloud to their wife, their mother. They show things getting worse, and everybody is frightened. You can feel it as you move around the camp.

Most frightened of all is Shazad Butt. Yesterday and today he is being very quiet. I would say *hooray* like Ruby Tanya when it is sausages for dinner, but Shazad's is the wrong kind of quiet, like the quiet between the wail of the siren and the coming of the planes. A *waiting* quiet. Mr Butt has the *Star*. I think he knows what his son has done, and I think Shazad knows he knows.

There is one good bit in the paper. It is written by the editor. My father reads it to my mother, who understands a little English but cannot read it. The editor says that sad things are happening in Tipton Lacey, but *Star* readers should not rush to judge others. What is true all over the world is true in the village also: that most people are good, most people are kind, most people want to help. There are a few who like to make trouble, and it is always these who have the loudest voices. The good people of Tipton Lacey must ignore the loud voices of the trouble-makers and listen to the little voice each of us has inside our head; the one that tells us what is right and what is wrong.

I like what the editor has written, says Mother, when Father was finished reading. You should snip it out and pin it to the board in the social club, with the best bits marked in red. Perhaps the loud voices among us will recognize themselves, and learn.

Oh, Mother, I hope so. I really, really do.

- Forty-five
Ruby Tanya

Saturday morning Mum and Dad had planned to drive to Danmouth for nets to go with the new curtains. I can never get over the exciting stuff grown-ups find to do. Anyway, because of their row yesterday Dad stalked out without breakfast and took the Volvo, marooning Mum at home. I was scared she might go by bus and take me along for company, but she didn't. She phoned her friend Penny and got a lift.

Don't go off, will you? she said as Penny pipped her horn. Your father's left his house keys and goodness knows when he'll be back. I'll only be a couple of hours.

Asra was still confined to camp, and I'd meant to phone Millie and suggest Danmouth mall. With that plan knocked on the head I decided I'd treat myself to a good old poke about, concentrating on Dad's office. There probably wouldn't be anything new since my last snoop, but you never know.

And I did come across something. It looked like nothing at first: a letter with ALBION PROPERTIES in big black print at the top. I assumed it'd be the usual waffle about planning applications and mortgages and heart-stopping stuff like that, but I skimmed it anyway and I'm glad I did, because this is what it said:

Dear Ed,

Further to the matter we discussed, and following your recent conversation with my associate Mr Cleaver, I am now in a position to place our agreement on a formal footing, as follows:

1. You will use your best endeavours, between now and next April, to create and co-ordinate opposition locally to the continued use of RAF Tipton Lacey as a camp for asylum seekers. My organization will assist wherever possible.
2. In the meantime my associates and myself will seek every opportunity to canvass support for your bid to be elected councillor for Tipton Lacey on Danmouth Town Council in next May's local elections.
3. I confirm that if everything goes according to plan, your agency will handle all sales-lettings of the very many properties my company plans to build at a certain location.
Yours sincerely,

The signature was an illegible ballpoint scrawl, but I didn't need to read it. There was only one guy who could have written this letter, and his name was Sefton Feltwell. I fed it through the fax machine to get a copy before replacing the original carefully in its folder. If I was my dad, I'd have kept that letter in the safe at my Danmouth office, but there you go: *Careless with fireworks, careless with everything.* That's an old saying I just made up.

- Forty-six
Ruby Tanya

I didn't know what I was going to do with my copy of
Feltwell's letter. I thought of showing it to Mum, but then it
occurred to me she might know all about it already. Just
because she and Dad argued all the time didn't mean they
had secrets from each other. I didn't want to go running to
PC Willoughby again: he'd think I couldn't wait to see my
dad behind bars. Besides, I wasn't sure Dad and Feltwell
were doing anything illegal. There's no law against protest-
ing, as long as you're not beating people up or setting their
homes on fire, and campaigning to have somebody elected
is part of the democratic process. It was that last bit, number
three, which I thought might be dodgy. Feltwell seemed to
be *bribing* Dad, offering to put a lot of business his way if he
stirred up enough trouble to . . . what?

I read paragraph three again. *If everything goes according to
plan*, it said. What was the plan? Why so coy about *a certain
location*, where very many properties were to be built?

A certain location. I sat on the sofa with the letter in my

115

lap, gazing through the sleet-spattered window at our privet hedge, shivering in the wind. I hoped the Volvo had broken down in some bleak, out-of-the-way spot where Dad couldn't get a signal on his phone, and that he was trudging along, hands in pockets, head down, trouser legs plastered to his shins. How sweet is that?

I wondered what Asra was doing. What *can* you do on a day like this, in a dilapidated wooden hut at the edge of a disused airfield where there's nothing but acre after acre of wet, wind-whipped grass and paths of crumbling concrete? There isn't even—

That's when it hit me: *a certain location*. Of *course*! RAF Tipton Lacey. Well, it *had* to be, didn't it? A huge expanse of land with nothing on it except the odd hangar and a cluster of rotting billets. Ideal for Feltwell's *very many properties*. Buy the place from the military for a song, bulldoze the old structures and Bob's your uncle: a ready-made building site. Only one fly in the ointment: those pesky asylum seekers. Get *them* out and away you go.

I still didn't know what to do. Though I hated to admit it, I needed an adult. Somebody who was on the asylum seekers' side, or at least not against them. It didn't take me long to decide who, because it was obvious. I'd show the letter to Gran.

Dad and Gran don't get on. She's an old hippy who wears beads and saves whales, and she threw my grandad Andrew out for eating her rabbit. She lives by herself now, in the old part of the village. Her cottage was built in 1779. Dad calls it the Hobbit Hole, which is the worst insult he can think of.

I couldn't go straight away in case Dad got back before Mum, though if you ask me it'd serve him right to have to stand in the sleet for a bit. I folded the letter, put it in my jeans pocket and switched on the telly.

116

- Forty-seven
Ruby Tanya

Hello, Gran.

Oh hi, Ruby, it's you. I wondered who it was knocking at this time of night. Nothing heavy, I hope?

Not really, Gran, just something I'd like you to take a look at.

Gran's the only person in the world who calls me Ruby. She knows why Dad christened me Ruby Tanya, and she doesn't approve. Patriotism is the last refuge of a scoundrel, she says. It's a quote, but I think she means Dad. It was nine o'clock: Mum only let me come because it's three weeks since Gran had a visit. Dad was still out when I set off.

Give me that jacket, love, I'll hang it by the radiator. You should wear a long coat, horrible night like this.

I haven't *got* a long coat, Gran, they're uncool. Did you have a long coat?

Oh yes, I had a beautiful Afghan with words embroidered in Elvish all round the hem. I'd have been warm at the South Pole in it. Come sit by the fire while I brew some green tea.

I don't really like green tea, but Gran doesn't buy ordinary tea and she never has coffee either. I can just about force the green stuff down if I think about something else. She brought two steaming mugs. There, she smiled, wrap your hands round that and you'll thaw out in no time. We sat either side of the ancient hearth, gazing into the flames which gave the room its only light. Gran's never in a rush, it's one of the things I like about her, but after a bit she smiled in the flickering glow and said, So, what d'you want me to look at, Ruby?

I put my half-empty mug on the hearthstone and produced the letter. This came to Dad from a guy called Sefton Feltwell, who's got something to do with—

Gran nodded. I know who Sefton Feltwell is, darling. I wondered who'd got him to come to the village. Might've known it'd be your father. Let's have a look.

I passed her the letter. You might need a light.

Naw. She shook her head. Firelight's plenty. She smoothed out the flimsy sheet and slanted it to catch the glow.

Hoooh! she went when she'd read it. If this means what it seems to mean, Ruby, it's heavy stuff. She shook her head again. So your dad fancies himself as a councillor, does he?

I dunno, Gran, he hasn't mentioned it in front of me.

No, I can see why he might not. Does your mum know?

I shrugged. Don't think so. Should I show this to someone? Who?

Who indeed? murmured Gran. She sat staring at the fire, dangling the letter between her knees. Won't he miss this, your dad?

It's a copy, from the fax machine. I put the original back.

Ah. She was silent for a while. I finished my tea, which was a relief, and settled back in the chair. It was snug, Gran's downstairs room. Restful. I closed my eyes.

Arthur Hadwin, said Gran.

Huh? I shook my head, yawning. Sorry, Gran, I must've nodded off. Who did you say?

Arthur Hadwin, Ruby. Editor of the *Star*. He's one of the good guys. I hung out at Frodo's with his dad.

Frodo's?

Bistro in Danmouth in the good old days. Went bust in 'seventy-nine, along with everything else. I reckon young Arthur ought to see this letter.

What d'you think he'll do with it?

Gran shrugged. I dunno, Ruby. He might start a campaign, Villagers Against Corruption: VAC for short.

Is Dad into corruption then, Gran? What'll happen to him?

It smells like corruption to me, love. Nothing'll happen to your dad if it can be stopped before it starts. Otherwise . . .

And what about me? I mean, Dad'll know how Mr Hadwin got the letter, won't he? He'll murder me, especially after I gave that flyer to Constable Willoughby.

Gran shook her head. He'll protect his source, will Arthur. I'll tell him he'd better. Your dad'll never suspect you Ruby, I promise. D'you trust me?

I smiled, nodded. Yes, I do, Gran, that's why I came here.

Then you can leave this with me. She folded the letter, put it under a hunk of coral on her side table and smiled in the firelight. More tea?

- Forty-eight
Ruby Tanya

It was nearly midnight when Dad came home, and I think he was a bit drunk because he sounded clumsier than usual, banging into things. I suppose that's what woke me up. Mum must've waited up for him. I could hear them talking. Not the words, just their voices.

I had to go to the bathroom. It wasn't an excuse to earwig, I really had to go. There were crockery sounds from the kitchen: Mum was getting Dad a bit of supper. As I tiptoed along the landing he came out of the front room to join her. *I'm not saying he did it, Sarah,* he boomed as he walked through.

Ssssh! went Mum. *You'll wake Ruby Tanya. We mustn't lay a thing like this on her.*

A thing like *what*? I crept to the banister, leaned over. The kettle was making so much din it was practically drowning them out. Mum said something like, *Why else would they have a giant picture of him, Ed? Raise their tankards to it, talk about killed in action?*

And Dad, in his *now I'm really starting to get mad* voice, said, I *told* you, Sarah, I don't *know*. Cleaver was cagey. I couldn't get a straight answer out of him. And now can we *please* drop it. I'm starving and you're not concentrating on that sandwich.

You're not concentrating on that sandwich. He can be a total prat, my dad. If *I* ever get married, which is unlikely, it won't be to someone who expects me to concentrate on his flipping sandwich, I can tell you that. Anyway, I didn't hear any more because somebody closed the kitchen door. I used the bathroom and went back to bed, where I lay wondering where Dad had been all day, why Cleaver was cagey and whose giant picture they'd toasted, whoever *they* were.

One thing was for sure: whatever they'd been discussing, Mum was dead set against me knowing about it, and of course that made me ultra curious. I was still playing and rewinding the bits I'd overheard inside my skull when I heard them coming up to bed. I squinted at the clock on my unit. It was five past one.

- Forty-nine
Asra

Sunday is foggy morning. We are shadows on the broken path, it makes us talk in whispers. The smallest children have not seen fog before. They make a game: it is to leave the path and be invisible to their parents. Mothers call their names, but the children are laughing somewhere and do not hear. It is not so good for the parents, this game.

At the mess it is damp and cold, even inside. Breakfast is eggs and bread. At my table we eat without talking. I am thinking to myself how slowly this day will pass, grey with English fog, and with fear that is all our own.

I am wrong. When we are making our way back, beside the shape of our hut is the shape of someone waiting. It is Ruby Tanya. I run to her. Ruby Tanya, I was not expect you today. How did you get in the gates?

She is laughing, hugging me. They let me in, Asra. I said I was here to see you and they opened the gate. Didn't expect 'em to, not in this fog, but there you go. What shall we do? Bus it into Danmouth?

No, interrupts my father. No Danmouth, nowhere outside the camp. He smiles at Ruby Tanya. I'm sorry, but Asra was beaten by some boys, you know this. You are welcome to be with my daughter in our home, or you can walk on the airfield, though I'm afraid it is not a nice morning.

Ruby Tanya nods. I understand, Mr Saber. She grins at me. Inside or out, Asra: you choose. I smile. I choose out, Ruby Tanya. Our home is full with just the three of us; with four it would be like ... *What* are the little fishes?

Sardines, says Ruby Tanya. Come on then. You can conduct me round the Saber Estate. 'Bye, Mr Saber, Mrs Saber.

Goodbye, Ruby Tanya, says Father. And remember: not beyond the airfield.

I guide my friend on the path to the airfield. It is long, and seems longer because we cannot see, but I don't care. I am with Ruby Tanya. We are alone together, the fog makes us more alone.

What will you show me first? says Ruby Tanya. She's speaking like a BBC lady. The deer park perhaps, or the orangery? Or what about the fountains?

I will show you first the ruins, I tell her.

Oooh! she squeals. I absolutely *adore* ruins, my dear. She thinks I am kidding, but I am not. There's no deer park, no orangery and no fountains, but there *are* ruins.

Somewhere the sun must have risen. A pearly light is seeping through the fog. Still we cannot see far, but the light makes me feel more happy. Or maybe Ruby Tanya is doing it, I don't know. We are on a long, cracked path with clumps of dying weeds; it is farther than I remember. Where are these divine ruins, my dear? she asks after a while. Still the BBC, but only half-joking, I think.

Close, I tell her, though I don't really know. In fact I am

beginning to feel lost, but luckily I spot what I have been looking for: a piece of rusty machinery in the long grass. Here we must leave the path, I tell her. From here, on an ordinary day I can see the ruins perfectly clearly, but today there's nothing. I have to hope I'm leading Ruby Tanya in the right direction.

We wade through the wet grass. My friend is getting fed up and I don't blame her: the legs of her jeans are wet and she thinks there are no ruins anyway. When I finally see them and point, she's amazed. There really *are* ruins, she gasps in her everyday voice. What was this place?

It used to be a farm, I tell her, but in the Second World War the government took all the land for an airfield and the farm died.

How d'you know? asks Ruby Tanya. I didn't know, and I was *born* in the village.

I smile sadly. Mr Shofiq read about it at the library in Danmouth. He says if we learn village history, we will fit in. I believe him before, but now I think it might not be enough.

No, murmured Ruby Tanya. It'd take an invasion from Mars to make some people see we're all Earthlings. Come on. Let's explore.

- Fifty
Ruby Tanya

So she's lived here about five minutes and she knows more about Tipton Lacey than I do. I must've passed the camp hundreds of times but I've never noticed any ruins, and I'd no idea it was once a farm. Just goes to show.

We approached the house, Asra leading. It felt dead spooky, but I suppose that was the fog. We crept through a gateway into what must once have been the farmyard. Hard now to imagine hens pecking about, the farmer's wife coming out of her kitchen to scatter corn for them. *What if her ghost is trapped here, doomed to feed a phantom flock for ever?* I shivered.

There was no porch door. You could see the place had been boarded up at one time, but somebody'd prised the planks loose and left them scattered about. Tramps, most likely. Come on, whispered Asra, there are lots of rooms. I will show you.

I hung back a bit. Been inside before, have you?

Oh yes, many times. It is my private place, when I'm

125

overfed of everybody.

It's fed up, not overfed.

Yes, fed up. Come on.

Are you sure the floors're safe?

I'm alive, Ruby Tanya, not lying dead inside.

OK, but let's not talk about *dead*.

It was foggy *inside*, which I hadn't expected, and there *were* a lot of rooms. Asra led me across stone-flagged floors, through doorways, down echoing passages. You could see where tramps had lit fires, some on hearths, one in the middle of a floor. There were a few empty bottles and some mildewed rags, but I could tell by the way the place smelled that nobody had dossed here lately.

Ready to go up? whispered Asra. We'd arrived at the foot of some dodgy-looking stairs.

Dunno, I murmured. Is there anything worth looking at?

Oh yes, she said. There is the bestest room, where I have my chair.

Your chair?

Well, it is mine now. Come on.

There were six rooms: five big ones and a little one. Asra's bestest was a big one at the front, where a frail wooden chair stood by the glassless window. When it is no fog, she told me, I can see from my chair right across the airfield to the huts. If Shazad Butt was coming, I would hide.

I glanced round the room. Where, under the chair? There's nowhere to hide, Asra.

She shook her head. Not in *here*, silly. Downstairs in the kitchen. Come, let me show you.

I let her lead me back to the kitchen, where my guided tour had begun. Now, she said, Shazad is crossing the yard. Where will you hide?

I dunno. Up the chimney?

She shrieked with laughter, setting off an echo that reminded me of an old movie I saw on telly, about a madwoman in an attic. Up the chimney, cackled Asra. You are comedian, Ruby Tanya.

Where, then? Now I'd remembered the madwoman, I was ready to leave.

In here, of course. She crossed to a row of windows that overlooked the farmyard. On the floor under them stood a long deep chest. I don't know why I hadn't noticed it before: it was the only thing in the room. She bent and lifted the heavy-looking lid, and of course the hinges creaked. I practically fudged my undies but Asra stayed cool – so cool that before I knew what was happening she'd stepped into the chest, squatted down and was lowering the lid. It was obviously she'd done it before.

OK, I croaked, I get the picture. Can we get out of here now, please?

She raised the lid and her eyebrows. Don't you want to try it? It's no sardines, plenty room for two.

N-no thanks, Asra. It's an ace hiding place, but I'd really rather be outside.

OK. She stepped out and let the lid fall with a mighty crash.

Aren't you scared when you're here by yourself? I asked as we headed for the door. The echo of the falling lid made me want to hurry.

Scared? she said. Why should I be scared? It's an old empty house, no planes come, no men with guns.

What about ghosts, though?

Ghosts? Asra pulled a face. I see ghosts, Ruby Tanya, but they do not live here, I bring them with me. They live inside my head, so for me everywhere is haunted.

I didn't know what to say to that.

- Fifty-one
Asra

It is good we had this time together, Ruby Tanya and me, because next day comes a bad thing: the baddest that could happen.

It is a letter for my father, from the government. It comes in the morning, but I do not know about it till afternoon because I am at school. It is a quiet day at school, no fighting. The pupils will put on a play for Christmas, *Joseph and the Amazing Technicolor Dreamcoat*, and we are learning our parts. I will be in chorus.

When I get home, Mother is weeping. Father is holding her. I am very scared. What is wrong? I ask.

There is a letter, says Father. It is the one we have waited for, but not the one we wanted. He shakes his head. The government says we must leave England, return to our country.

But *why*, Father? I cry. We have made no troubles and *I* can't go: I'm in the play.

Play?

Yes, the Christmas play, at school.

Ah. He smiles sadly. I don't think the government will change its mind because of a play, Asra. We have ten days to appeal.

We will be *killed* in our country, sobs Mother. Do they know that, Gul? Do they *know*?

Hush, Nusrat, murmurs Father, you will frighten the child. Of *course* they know, I wrote it on the form.

Then how can they—?

Sssh! He is rocking Mother like a baby. *I* don't know, Nus. I have no answers to your questions: they are my questions too. Who knows how the mind of a government works? He laughs, short like a bark. Perhaps it has no mind, just programs like a computer.

Will they come with guns, Father, to drive us away?

He shakes his head. I think not, Asra, unless we refuse to move.

Will we refuse? *Can* we? I will refuse because of the play.

He smiles, a tired smile. No, my dear one, you will not, because it would change nothing. We will continue to behave as we have always behaved, so that whatever happens, nobody will say of us, *It is their own fault, they brought it on themselves.*

At the mess everybody is looking to the Sabers, because the blow they all fear has fallen on us. They are not glad it isn't them. They are thinking, *You now, us later.* The fear has thickened.

When I have gone to bed, two people come to talk to my parents. They are from an organization that helps asylum seekers with their appeals. They talk softly, I don't hear anything they say, I hope it is something nice, because I don't want to be a goat again, and I don't want us to die.

- Fifty-two
Ruby Tanya

When Asra told me first thing Tuesday I couldn't believe it. I was like, *Why?* How come guys like Shazad Butt get to stay and you have to go? It's crazy.

She didn't say much, she was too upset. In fact she snuggled her face in my neck and was having a good cry when the buzzer went.

First lesson, Asra couldn't stop sniffling. When she told Ms Rule why, she let her go to the first-aid room where she'd at least have a bit of privacy. She's all right, old Rule. Golden, us kids call her. *Golden Rule*, geddit?

I was working with Millie. She goes, What's up with your friend? I told her and she said, If it was me I wouldn't go.

Is that right? I said. What *would* you do?

Run off, she says. Hide.

Yeah, right. I didn't say anything else, I didn't feel like it, but she'd started me thinking.

Asra showed up for second lesson, holding herself together. At break I steered her into the doorway of the sports store, took her by the shoulders and gazed into her eyes. Listen: what'd happen if it was the last day, time for your mum and dad to set off to the airport and they couldn't find you?

She sniffled, shook her head. I don't know, Ruby Tanya. What *would* happen?

They'd miss their flight, and there might not be another till next day, and that might be full. And even if it wasn't, they couldn't get on if you were still missing.

But I *won't* be missing, Ruby Tanya, I will be with them. Let's talk about something else.

It's not just talk, Asra, it's a plan. I've thought about it, and I think it'd work.

No. She shook her head. You want to be kind but is not so good, this plan. Suppose my parents missed their flight; suppose they missed two flight, or ten. It would change nothing. The government would find me in the end, and then they'd send us away, a few days late, but the bad men are patient, they would be waiting. She smiled, a watery smile. You want to help, I know, but you are not the government.

Asra – I squeezed her thin shoulders – don't give up, please. Remember Sunday, the ruins? Nobody knows you go there. You could hide and I'd bring stuff from home, blankets and things. You'd be all right, you said the place didn't scare you. I'd bring you food, stuff to drink. You could borrow my Walkman, even my phone. Say you'll think about it at least.

The ruins, she murmured, smiling with her eyes. You have been such a friend, Ruby Tanya, how can I say no to you? Yes, I will think about it, but you must think too. Think about your father, who hates our people. You would be stealing his things to help me, to keep my parents here. What would he do if he caught you? And you would be hiding a runaway, someone hunted by the government with dogs, helicopters; even satellites. They would be sure to find me sooner or later, and you could be sent to prison. She looked me in the eye. I will think, Ruby Tanya, and so must you. Then we will talk again.

I wasn't a star pupil that day. Couldn't concentrate for picturing Asra a week or two from now, in Mr Younis's class. Would *he* let her go to the first-aid room?

- Fifty-three
Asra

It is difference already, this room which has been our home. It looks difference because Mother has packed things already: there are spaces on shelves and in corners. And it feels difference because soon we will leave with our cases and never return.

I stand looking at the changes and Mother says, Come, I have something to tell you. She is sitting on the bed because we have no soft chairs. I go to her, she puts her arm round me. Father and I need you to be very brave, she says.

Fear flickers inside me. I look at her. Why brave, Mother?

She squeezes gently. We are looking for a way to keep you safe from the bad men, Asra.

I frown. Which bad men, Mother? A picture is in my head: the rude man at Mayfields.

The bad men in our country, dear one.

In our country? I don't understand, how can you . . . ?

By not taking you there.

You mean, we might not have to go?

She smiles sadly. *You*, Asra. *You* might not have to go. Those people – the two who were here last night – they will try to get permission for you to stay with a family here in—

No! I pull away, horrified. Not without you, I cry. You and Father. I will stay with you, in our country or anywhere. I don't *want* another family, I'd rather . . . I'd rather be a *goat*.

Asra, says Father, who has entered silently, this is the one opportunity your mother and I will have to ensure your safety. It will be a hundred times easier for us to face what must be faced, if we know our enemies cannot reach you. Don't you *want* to make it as easy as possible for your mother?

I . . . of *course* I do, Father, but . . .

Then be *brave*, my precious one. He comes to me, scoops me up, rocks me. Oh, Asra, we don't *want* to leave you, surely you know that? It might not happen anyway, but if it does, your safety will be the one glimmer of happiness in our unhappy situation.

I make myself stop crying. Father dabs away my tears with his handkerchief, tells me I'm his big brave daughter and holds my hand all the way to the mess. I don't feel like anybody's big brave daughter. I eat like a sparrow, and when I go to bed my head is aching. *Don't you want to make it as easy as possible for your mother?* Flipping trick question, as Ruby Tanya would say.

- Fifty-four
Ruby Tanya

I did a lot of moping over Asra that week, mostly at home. At school I hadn't time to mope, what with end of term exams, *Joseph*, and preparations for the reopening of the shared area next Tuesday. Talk about everything coming at once. The mayor of Danmouth would grace the reopening with his presence. Tipton Lacey doesn't have its own mayor, just a moron. The Moron of Tipton Lacey, otherwise known as my dad. Anyway, we'd be doing a bit of choral speaking for the mayor, and I bet he couldn't wait. It was a poem about a guy who lays down his life for his friends, which Ramsden chose because that's what Mr Conway did. Usually us kids'd have sent anything of that sort up so ruthlessly as to make it impossible to teach, but this time nobody did. We wouldn't have dreamed of it, which is weird in a way.

I'm not saying I never thought of Asra at school; of course I did. For one thing I felt desperately sorry for her, sitting exams she'd never get the results of, rehearsing Christmas stuff when she'd be a thousand miles away by Christmas, in a country where they don't have it. *If* she was still alive, that is. You bet I thought about her.

Dad was in a mood all week as well, like a bear with a sore bum, and it didn't help when he scanned the *Star* at Friday breakfast. That was another thing that'd preyed on my mind: had Gran passed Feltwell's letter on to Arthur Hadwin and if so, what use would he make of it? I'd pictured a big black headline with Dad's name, and when I heard the paper drop I concentrated very hard on my mini-wheats. But it wasn't like that. Nothing on the front page. Rather than make a news story out of it, Hadwin had written a piece himself, an editorial, on the centre spread. I'd told myself Gran hadn't passed on the letter, that there was nothing in the paper at all, and was relaxing with a slice of toast and marmalade when Dad found Hadwin's piece.

He roared. Flung the paper in the air, where it came apart, fluttering down to lie in overlapping sheets on the quarry tiles.

Mum, who was topping up her cup, topped up the sugar bowl instead. What on *earth*'s the matter, Ed? she cried.

It's not me, bellowed Dad, it's *him*. Hadwin. He's always been against me, what I'm trying to do here, and now he's done a hatchet job on me, destroyed my character. It's libel, I'll take him to the cleaner's, sue him for every penny he's got. I'll close his rotten little paper once and for all.

Mum carried the sugar bowl to the sink, tipped out the syrupy contents and asked, Has Hadwin used your name, Ed?

No, he ruddy well hasn't, but he might as well have. *Well-known local property dealer. Prominent in the campaign to have asylum seekers accommodated elsewhere.* Who else could he be referring to, Sarah? And how in the blazes did he get hold of the information?

It's not libel if he hasn't named you, Ed, said Mum reasonably. You won't be able to sue. She bent down, gathered the paper page by page. What is it anyway? What's the information he's got? Does it really matter?

Of *course* it matters, you daft cow. It's confidential business. It doesn't break any laws and it's *our* affair, mine and Feltwell's; nobody else's.

What an opera. For once I was glad when it was time to go to school. I didn't get to read Hadwin's editorial till I got back that afternoon. Mum'd read it and was grimly quiet. You won't like it, Ruby Tanya, she told me as I opened the centre spread, but she didn't try to stop me.

It was a good piece of writing. Clever, in that it alerted the villagers to the tacky stuff that seemed to be going on behind the scenes, without openly accusing anybody of anything. I had to agree with Dad on one point though: nobody in Tipton Lacey could fail to recognize him as one of Hadwin's villains.

Which left me hoping fervently that Gran was right when she said the editor would protect his source.

- Fifty-five
Ruby Tanya

It was a tense weekend at our house. Dad's foul mood continued, and he fratched with Mum at every opportunity. It took him all his time to speak to me, so that I began to think he'd found out about the letter. It was Asra's last weekend, and I was determined to spend as much time with her as possible. I decided to be open about it instead of pretending I was meeting Millie or something. Dad didn't bother hiding the fact that he was glad the Sabers were being sent home, so I didn't see why I should lie to keep him happy. It was scary, announcing first thing Saturday that I was off to the camp, but all he said when I told him was, suit yourself.

It was tense in the Saber household too, of course. Asra's folks were OK with me but in a detached sort of way, as though I was already part of their past. I said the only thing there was to say, that I was very sorry they had to leave, that I was going to miss Asra very much, that I'd never forget them.

We walked on the airfield, just the two of us. The Sabers

would fly out next Saturday, 4 December. I'd been working on Asra at school, trying to get her to give my plan a go, but I hadn't been able to budge her. It's a bad plan, she'd insisted, brought a long way. You mean far-fetched, I'd smiled, and she'd said, Thank you, Ruby Tanya, but there is no rush for me to learn good English now.

So I was unprepared when, as soon as nobody could overhear, she said, We will do it.

Do what?

Your plan: the far-fetched one.

You mean you'll— I stopped dead, gaping.

She nodded. Close your mouth, please. Yes, I will hide in the ruins. My parents tried to put me with a family here, but there was no permission. They want me to stay, so I will stay. This way, maybe they will stay too.

Brilliant! I yelled.

Ssssh! Asra glanced back. It won't be so brilliant if somebody hears us.

We headed for the ruins. There was no fog today, so they came in sight when we were only halfway there. I looked back to make sure nobody could see where we were going and it was all right: the hut roofs were on the horizon. It was important now that Asra's secret hideaway should stay secret.

My heart was pounding. The first flush of excitement was over, and I was beginning to realize what I'd taken on. Asra wouldn't stay in the ruins tonight of course: she'd do a runner on the night of 3 December, but before then we'd need to get the place ready. That meant bedding, food and water, a torch, candles and matches and all sorts of other stuff, to be smuggled in without anybody seeing. Without my parents noticing stuff was missing. Planning all this was going to be an awesome task, never mind actually *doing* it.

And we'd six days, starting now.

- Fifty-six
Ruby Tanya

We sat, me on the windowsill, Asra on her chair, and made a start. First up, getting the stuff. Everything is higgledy-piggledy in our room, said Asra. She'd once heard somebody say higgledy-piggledy at school and liked the sound of it. After making sure it wasn't a bad word, she'd adopted it. Some of our things are packed, she said, and some are not. I think I can take a few bits without my parents noticing, but nothing big like blankets, because I have to go through the Butts' room.

Yeah, I said, bedding's going to be a problem all right. I'm not sure how I'll get it out of *our* place without anybody seeing me, or noticing it's gone.

Maybe I can manage without bedding, Ruby Tanya.

What? I looked at her. It's going to be December, you div. You can't sleep uncovered, you'd die in the night. Anyway, I've just had an idea.

What?

Well, what if we didn't *have* to smuggle the bedding past

our folks?

I don't understand. *Do* you mean *buy* it, at a shop?

Good lord, no. What d'you think I am, a millionaire? No, I was thinking about Gran. My grandma.

Steal from your grandmother?

No, Asra, not steal. I bet if I told Gran what we're doing and why, she'd lend us some stuff, and not just blankets. She might get us everything we need.

Oh, Ruby Tanya, d'you *think* so? It would be very brill.

I grinned. Very, *very* brill, that'd be. I'll go see her tonight. Now, the next problem's getting stuff past the guys who man your gates.

Asra smiled, shook her head. We won't have to.

Why not?

Mushroom Gap.

What you on about, Asra? What's Mushroom Gap when it's at home?

She chuckled. When it's at home, it is a place where peoples have made the fence flat so they can pick mushrooms on the airfield. When it is *not* at home, I don't know what it is. You must go to the end of Glebe Lane and turn right into Long Lane.

I nodded. I know it, it goes behind the school.

Yes, and when it comes to the airfield, that is where the fence is flat.

Now *that*'s what I call dead convenient. What's next?

We plotted and schemed till nearly lunch time. I wanted us to skip lunch, stay here in the ruins, but Asra wouldn't. Father will worry, she said. Maybe he will search for me, and if he finds me here . . .

I nodded. I see what you mean. I'm still thinking it's our last weekend but it isn't, is it? Not any more. Shall I come tomorrow, let you know how I got on with Gran?

Yes, my parents will expect you. We must do what is expected, so they won't suspect. Come on.

We sauntered back across the airfield. I tried to picture it in a year or two's time if Sefton Feltwell had his way, crammed with tawdry, overpriced houses on streets with silly names.

And Asra's folk? Forgotten like the mushrooms.

- Fifty-seven
Ruby Tanya

Hi, Gran.

Hi, yourself. Did you see the piece in the *Star*?

Yes.

What did your father think?

He's out for blood. I hope it won't be mine.

Don't worry, sweetheart, I told you: Hadwin's never dobbed anyone in and never will. Is that why you're here?

Well no, Gran, not exactly. I . . . I was hoping you might help with another problem I've got.

At your age, Ruby, you should have no problems. What is it?

We sipped green tea and I told her about the Sabers. She listened without interrupting, and when I'd finished she shook her head.

Sheeesh! That's heavy stuff to lay on *anybody*, child, let alone a poor old crone like me. Still, a trouble shared is a trouble halved, as the saying goes. She chuckled. It's a lie, but that's how it goes. At the risk of being a drag, I have to say I doubt whether the powers that be'll postpone the parents' deportation because their kid's missing. They'd have to have a heart to care about a detail like that, and they haven't.

I looked at her. We've got to *try* though, Gran – Asra and me. We can't just let her go. I'm hoping maybe if Asra stays free for a while, they might give her a whatsit – amnesty.

Hah! Gran swallowed the last of her tea. The optimism of youth, Ruby. Still, I agree we've got to try.

We?

Oh yes, your old gran's on board, sweetheart. Anything that screws up those gangsters at Westminster has *got* to be worth doing. She gazed at me. Why don't you bring your friend *here*? She can crash in the spare room: better than that old ruin.

Oh no, we *couldn't* Gran. If they found her here you'd go to jail.

You're risking it.

I'm a kid, they'll go easy on me. What I hope you'll do is lend us stuff – blankets and that – so we don't have to smuggle everything past our parents.

Gran nodded. Anything you want, sweetheart, and I mean *anything*. D'you want stuff now, tonight?

Oh no, Gran, not tonight. How about half-ten tomorrow morning?

No problem. And remember, if that ruin gets too cold for your friend, floor too hard or whatever, fetch her here. It's a long time since I laid my scrawny neck on the block in a good cause; too long.

Grans. You should be able to get 'em on the National Health.

– Fifty-eight
Ruby Tanya

It could hardly have been a worse day, weather-wise. I woke to the rattle of rain on my window, a booming wind. Just what you need on a cross-country bedding hump.

Breakfast was a quiet affair. Mum and Dad were being frosty with each other again. Nobody tells me what's going on of course, but I gathered there was to be a public meeting that Dad would address and Mum didn't approve. I guessed it had something to do with Dad standing for election. I wasn't interested; all I cared about was getting out of the house and on with what I had to do.

And of course they gave me a hard time. Where does she think she's going? growled Dad to Mum as I fetched my coat.

Your father wants to know where you're going, says Mum.

Tell him I'm off out, Mum.

She's going out, Ed.

I can see that. It's ten o'clock Sunday morning, pouring

down, blowing a gale and your daughter's going out. Think that's a good idea, do you?

Mum shook her head. Not particularly, Ed, but then I don't think your public meeting's a good idea either.

What the heck's *that* got to do with your daughter trailing about in wet clothes, catching pneumonia?

She's your daughter too, Ed. If there's something you want to say to her, I'm sure she'll listen.

Are you? Are you really?

Blah, blah, blah, blah, blah. It went on and on – I won't bore you with it. I managed to escape in the end, but it was ten to eleven when I got to Gran's.

She was brilliant. She'd packed blankets in a battered rucksack so nobody'd know what I was carrying, and there was a bulging haversack as well. Torch in there, she said. Also matches, candles, aspirins, scissors, a pocket knife, string, a towel, chocolate, pressed dates, bottled water and a polybag big enough for your friend to sleep in, keep draughts out. Oh, and a few personal items, just in case.

Like I said, brilliant. I didn't wait for green tea but set off, loaded like one of those mules you see in Spain. I had to go through part of our estate to reach Long Lane, and that's where the foul weather helped. On a fine Sunday all the sads come out and shampoo their Volvos, and some of them know me. It's likely I'd have been asked where I was going, loaded up like that. Some wally might even have bumped into Dad in the pub and mentioned it. As it was I reached the puddly, unmade track called Long Lane without seeing another human being. A hundred years ago Long Lane was the road to Danmouth, but nobody uses it now, especially on days like this. It's two miles to the camp, but at least I knew I wasn't going to run into some busybody along the way.

Pain in the bum, busybodies.

- Fifty-nine
Asra

I am glad it is raining. I can wear my long coat to breakfast.
It has two big pockets. In one pocket is soap, my toothbrush,
some scissors, a hairbrush and a comb. In the other is some
hankies, one vest and two knickers. These things I will take
to the ruins after breakfast, while Father and Mother are
busy at the social club with Mr Shofiq, who is helping with
our appeal.

Breakfast is porridge, which I hate, and toast, which I like.
When nobody is looking I slip a knife and a spoon and some
little pats of butter in my purse, with a handful of sugar
cubes.

Away from the buildings is very horrible, rain and wind. I
wear my scarf over my mouth and nose and pull down my
woolly hat. Only my eyes can be seen, but is nobody to see
them. The wind blows me sideways. I don't think so Ruby
Tanya will come today.

At the ruins is still, I can rest from the rain and wind. In
the kitchen I open the chest, pull the things from my pockets

and lay them on the floor of it, on a supermarket bag. Everything is a bit wet, but will come dry soon. I put in the things from my purse as well. Then I go upstairs and sit on my chair by the window with my coat and scarf off. I feel cold, but better cold here than hot in my country, where are the bad men. I look at my watch: it is ten o'clock.

Rain blows in sheets across the airfield. If I could take this weather to my country, our people would grow fat. All this good water, falling out of the sky. How the grain would swell, and the cattle. How the children would dance, in the mud that once was dust. *If only*, as Ruby Tanya would say.

I sit and watch the rain till nearly half past twelve, then start to put on my coat. Soon it will be lunch at the mess. Mother and Father will expect me there. I must be careful to do all they expect, till Friday. I am winding the damp scarf round my face when I hear my name.

Asra, are you there? It's me.

I clatter downstairs, raising dust. Ruby Tanya, I thought you would not come. She has big load, like donkeys in my country. Everything is dripping on the floor.

Course I've come. I *said* I would, didn't I? She shrugs off her straps, dumps a fat pack on the flags, a smaller one beside it. You should see what Gran's put in these, Asra. You'll be snug as a bug in a rug.

I'm snug as a bug in a rug *now*, I cry. I don't know what is meaning, *snug as a bug in a rug*, but I like it. It sounds even gooder than *higgledy-piggledy*.

– Sixty
Ruby Tanya

I got a shock Monday morning. Dad'd gone off to work, Mum was lingering over her second coffee and I was sitting there feeling smug because everything had gone so smoothly yesterday. At ten past eight I stretched, yawned and said, Well, better go get ready, I suppose.

Mum nodded. Me too.

I looked at her. I didn't know you were at the shop this morning.

She shook her head. I'm not, I'm coming with you.

To *school*?

Yes.

What for? *She's found out about me and Asra: our plan.*

Because ... sit down a minute, Ruby Tanya, I've something to tell you.

I *had* to sit, my legs had gone all rubbery. What?

Mum sighed. I don't know if this is the right thing, love. I've thought and thought about it, and all I can think to do is mention it to Mr Ramsden.

149

Mention *what*, Mum? She looked worried, scared even.

It's . . . it's about tomorrow. You know, the reopening, with the mayor and everything?

Yes, what about it?

We can't let it go ahead, Ruby Tanya. I mean, the reopening part's all right, it's the *name*. We mustn't let them use that name. *His* name.

What, the mayor? D'you mean the *mayor's* name, Mum? *She's flipped her lid*, I thought.

She shook her head. No, of *course* not the mayor, darling. *Him*. Stuart Conway.

Why, what's wrong with his name? Why mustn't we . . . ?

Because he wasn't carrying that bomb out of the school, Ruby Tanya; he was carrying it *in*.

You could've knocked me down with a feather. That's what they say, isn't it? I've always thought it a really daft expression, but I know what they mean now. I felt weightless, like Mum's words had switched off gravity so that a puff of air might blow me clean away.

Next thing I remember was Mum holding a glass of water to my lips. Come on, sweetheart, she coaxed. Have a few sips, you'll feel better in a minute. I did, and I did, but it was a while before I could get myself together to leave the chair. Meanwhile Mum stood behind me stroking my hair, murmuring, *Stupid, stupid, stupid woman*. She meant herself, for telling me like that.

I don't know whether she made Ramsden faint as well, but he put in a couple of hasty phone calls and sent a note round. Exactly what the note said I don't know: it was teachers' eyes only. Rule just announced that tomorrow's reopening was postponed, though the shared area would in fact be available. As she was speaking, I remembered something I'd heard while eavesdropping on my parents last Saturday night. Mum's voice, half drowned by the kettle: *Why else would they have a giant picture of him, Ed? Raise their tankard to it?*

Now I knew whose giant picture she was referring to.

- Sixty-one
Ruby Tanya

Time for something a bit more cheerful, yeah? I think so. I didn't know about this till after, of course, but while all the nasty stuff was happening in Tipton Lacey, a small miracle was taking place at Danmouth Infirmary.

It was Asif Akhtar and Keith Allardyce. The staff didn't know it was Allardyce who'd put Akhtar there, or that somebody had cut Allardyce's feet to avenge Akhtar. So, not only did they have them in the same ward, they put them *next* to each other.

Asif was dozing when they wheeled Keith in. He woke up just as a nurse drew back the curtain that separated his bed from the next, which had been empty since yesterday. When he saw who was in it, he thought his medication was making him hallucinate. Allardyce hadn't seen him so Asif quickly turned away, hurting his ribs in the process. He lay with his back to the other boy, the sheet pulled up round his ears, pretending to be asleep.

Trouble is, you can't stay like that in hospital. They don't let you. There's always somebody coming round taking your temperature, checking your blood pressure, asking if you've moved your bowels. Asif hadn't been on his side five minutes when a nurse appeared, asking in a bright voice that very question. I haven't moved *anything*, he muttered into the pillow. I *daren't*. Go away.

She didn't go away. They don't. Instead she pulled back the sheet and helped him sit up. She was drawing his curtain when Allardyce recognized him. *You*, he gasped. What *you* doing here, you creepazoid?

You should know, growled Asif just before the bright fabric came swishing between them.

The nurse smiled. You two know each other? Asif nodded with a sickly grin. That's nice, she chirped. You'll be able to keep each other amused.

Oh sure, thought Asif. *He's amused me once already, that's why I'm here. Maybe he'll kick the rest of my ribs in today, really get me laughing.*

When he'd finished with the bedpan, the nurse opened the curtain and strode off. The other boy glared. Your stink was bad enough at school, Akhtar; it's worse in here. Why the heck did they have to put me next to you?

Well it wasn't 'cos I requested it, shot back Asif, embarrassed by the business with the bedpan. What you here for anyway?

One of your lot stuck blades through my trainers – my feet're like mince.

Not one of *my* lot.

Yes, and I know which one.

Who, then?

Never mind. I'm gonna grab a ziz now, so quit the rabbit. He rolled over, pulled up the sheet and went to sleep.

At half six Asif's mum and dad came to see him. Keith

Allardyce was awake, but he kept his back turned as they found chairs, settled themselves either side of their son's bed and chatted to him in their own language. He couldn't help wondering what they'd do if they knew his attacker lay in the next bed.

When his own parents arrived a few minutes later, Mr Akhtar nodded to Allardyce senior, who nodded back. It was a perfunctory greeting, but Keith was surprised his father had responded at all. He was always going on about how he hated asylum seekers, telling his wife and son and anybody else who'd listen what he'd do to every one of them if he had his way. The two women exchanged shy smiles, and Keith wondered what'd happen if he told Mrs Akhtar his dad would love to boil her in oil. Would Dad deny it?

Our son was beaten up, volunteered Mr Akhtar. At school.

Oh, said Mr Allardyce. That's rough.

Disgusting, added his wife.

What is the matter with *your* son?

Keith's dad grimaced. Somebody put knives in his shoes, cut his feet to ribbons. That was at school as well.

How terrible. Did they catch the person responsible?

No.

Pity. Such a one deserves the severest punishment, like the boy who beat Asif.

Mr Allardyce nodded. I know what *I'd* do if I caught 'em: string 'em up by their thumbs and let 'em dangle till they begged for mercy. They'd not do it again.

I would take a stick, growled Akhtar senior. Beat them senseless.

Asif looked at Keith, who seemed a bit pale. Keith swallowed and looked away.

I'm not sure that's the best way, ventured Keith's mother. You know what they say: *Violence begets violence.*

154

You are so right, nodded Mrs Akhtar. Those boys, they come from bad homes, I think. Homes full of ignorance and stupidity. Our sons are lucky – at least we are bringing them up decently.

The four parents chatted happily, ignoring the boys till it was time to go. When they'd gone, Keith looked at Asif. Hey, cheers – y'know, for not . . .

Asif nodded. You're ugly, Allardyce, but you'd look even uglier dangling by your thumbs. Anyway, it's not *your* fault: you come from a home full of ignorance and stupidity.

Yes, but hey, grinned Keith, doesn't every kid you know?

- Sixty-two
Ruby Tanya

I was becoming a fixture up the camp, spending as much time as I could with Asra. There wasn't even a problem with Dad any more. He knew the Sabers were going. It wasn't worth the hassle trying to keep us apart. I was biking up there after tea Monday when I saw the banner.

It was a massive thing, fastened to two trees and stretched right across the road so everyone heading for Danmouth had to drive under it. On it, in great red capitals, were the words DANGER – ASYLUM SEEKERS AHEAD.

It wasn't there yesterday. It probably wasn't there this morning: if the camp bus had driven under it somebody would surely have mentioned it at school. I passed it and stopped to look back. The message on the other side was ALIEN BRATS GO HOME.

I knew who'd done it of course. I don't mean Dad had actually driven out here with a set of ladders and put it up himself, but he'd had the thing made. I recognized the style, which was exactly like the boards he used in his work –

boards that said FOR SALE, UNDER OFFER, SOLD. The guys who made those for him had made this as well.

I felt deeply ashamed, especially of ALIEN BRATS GO HOME, because it was obviously there for the camp kids to read as they were driven to school. It reminded me of Asra's story about Mr Younis and the goat-children. And I'd told her it couldn't happen here.

I didn't mentioned it to the Sabers, just like I didn't tell them about Stuart Conway. They had fresh troubles of their own anyway: their appeal had been turned down, which meant the police could show up at any time and take them to the airport; they might not wait till Saturday. The uncertainty meant the family couldn't plan their packing properly: anything that couldn't be packed now, such as the bedding they were using and clean clothes for tomorrow, would have to be abandoned if the Sabers were removed without notice. It also threatened *our* plan, mine and Asra's, because we could no longer count on having till Friday night for Asra to vanish. Her parents knew nothing of this, of course.

It was too cold for a stroll on the airfield, so Asra took me to the social club. We went in the TV room, where a few people sat in battered armchairs watching the news. The newsreader was asking some expert how embarrassed the government was about asylum seekers. If he'd been asking me I'd have said, *Not nearly as embarrassed as it ought to be*.

We left the TV room and found a table in a place that had a few board games, some second-hand books and a hot drinks dispenser. We got coffees and I showed Asra how Snakes and Ladders works. I used a two-pence for a counter because there was only one tiddlywink. Asra was tickled by the word tiddlywink, but really we were only pretending to enjoy ourselves. It's hard to get absorbed in Snakes and Ladders when real life's reduced to a game of chance.

- Sixty-three
Asra

A good game, Snakes and Ladders. If I knew I would stay here in England with my parents, how happy I would be, playing it with Ruby Tanya. How funny *tiddlywink* would sound. But I am not happy at all, because there is a thing I must tell to my friend before we part tonight. I shake a five, slide my *tiddlywink* to the last square and win the game. Now; I will tell her now.

Asra?

What? She has spoken first, I must wait.

I'm sorry, Asra, but I have to warn you about something – something my dad's done.

What has he done, Ruby Tanya? *What can he do to me now?*

There's a banner, a nasty message across the road. You'll see it on your way to school tomorrow.

Say it *now*. I . . . will not see it, Ruby Tanya, because I can't come to school any more.

You . . . What d'you mean, you *can't*. It's Tuesday tomorrow, you've got till Friday.

We don't know that, Ruby Tanya, not now. My father says, What if police come while you are at school, we might have to go without you. So he will keep me at home.

But they'll be going without you *anyway*, Asra. Our plan . . .

Of course, but my father knows nothing of our plan. And it may have to change.

Ruby Tanya nods. I know – you might have to do it before Friday, if they come for you. You *will* still do it though, won't you? Everything's ready.

I nod. I will do it if I can; if they don't come when I'm asleep. Listen.

What?

If you come tomorrow, or Wednesday or Thursday, and they tell you my parents have been taken, come to the ruins. I will be there. Don't use the gates, walk away and come through Mushroom Gap. If I am not there, you will know they caught me sleeping.

And sent me to the bad men, who will make me sleep for ever.

– Sixty-four
Ruby Tanya

I don't think it was my imagination: the camp kids *were* quieter than usual that Tuesday morning. In the yard, I mean. Oh, I tried to tell myself it was the Sabers' plight getting to them, or the fact that we'd been done out of today's little ceremony, but I knew it was ALIEN BRATS GO HOME really. They wouldn't be hearing from the mayor today but they'd heard from the Moron of Tipton Lacey, loud and clear.

The village was going to hear from him too. He'd had an e-mail last night from Sefton Feltwell to say they'd got the village hall for a public meeting on 6 December. He was so chuffed he brought the printout downstairs to show me and Mum. Here we go, he crowed; the launching of Ed Redwood, Monday 6 December at seven-thirty p.m. He smiled complacently and added, *Councillor* Redwood after the May elections, no danger. He's so thick-skinned, he hasn't twigged Mum's not one hundred per cent behind his drive for an ethnically cleansed village with a Britain First councillor.

Anyway, he'd made a good start depressing the camp kids with his banner. Ramsden'd seen it on his way in – he drives that way. He didn't mention it in so many words, but when we assembled in the hall and he declared the shared area open, he asked us to notice the word *shared*. All of Tipton Lacey is a shared area, he said. It belongs to everybody who lives here, and everybody who lives here belongs to *it*. There have been no sightings of alien craft over Tipton Lacey. Kids who hadn't seen the banner probably thought he'd fallen out of his pram, but I thought it was good.

He didn't say anything at all about Stuart Conway.

At morning break I had a falling-out with Millie. I only wanted to walk round the yard with her, but when I said, Hi, she was like, You only want me 'cos your precious Asra's not here, so you can sod off.

I didn't say a word, just spun on my heel and left, telling myself she was a touchy cow who wasn't worth bothering with. Later, when I'd had time to think about it, I had to admit she was right in a way. It can't be all that flattering to be somebody's second-best friend. I promised myself I'd make it up to her if she'd let me.

But I'd soon be too busy to fret over Millie Ross. As the buzzer brought break to an end, the police were swooping on the Sabers.

- Sixty-five
Asra

You can expect something and still be shocked when it happens. I am helping Mother sort some things for packing when Mrs Butt screams and the curtain is ripped down. There are four policemen. Mother jumps up with a cry as they come towards us. Where's your husband? demands one.

Father is at the social club, still trying with Mr. Shofiq to find a way for us to stay. Mother murmurs, Fetch your father, Asra.

No! The policeman shakes his head. She stays. Where is he?

The social club.

Perkins, Toller.

Sir?

Double over there. Don't bring him here, go straight to the van. You. He looks to Mother. Gather whatever you're taking with you. You've got five minutes.

But I cannot carry . . .

We'll carry, you just get it together. He looks to me. Help your mother.

Mother starts dragging bags and cases to the middle of the room. She is weeping softly. The two policemen stand with their arms folded, watching. I don't think so they feel sorry for her. I am sorry, because in one minute I will add to her sadness.

I look to one of the policemen. Please?

What is it?

I need toilet.

Tch! Where is it?

Through there. I nod to the blanket that separates our room from the next. The hut's two toilets are in a little room at the end, with the shower.

He nods. All right. Go with her, Les. I lift the blanket, drop it in front of Les's face. Mr and Mrs Majid have listened, they know what is happening. Delay him, I say in our language.

When Les ducks under the blanket I am halfway across the room, running. *Oi!* He is so busy looking to me he does not see Mr Majid crouching under his feet. He trips and crashes to the floor as I go under the next curtain.

In this room a mother is feeding her baby. Her mouth falls open as I dash through. There are no more blankets, just the bathroom door on the left and the exit straight in front. I go for the exit.

I am outside, but I don't know how close is Les. On the airfield is nowhere to hide. If I run there he will catch me easily. At the edge of the path is a row of wheelie bins. I run to them, duck behind. Les bursts out of the hut and stands panting, looking round. There are other huts – I could be in one of them, or behind, or between. He doesn't know what to do. I watch, breathing quietly. He decides, strides to the

163

next hut, goes inside. I find a bin that is only half full and climb in, letting its lid rest on my head so there's a slot I can see out of. If Les comes I will bury myself under the rubbish I am standing in, but I hope he won't come.

It stinks.

- Sixty-six
Asra

This is what I see from my wheelie bin. First Les comes out, talking to his radio. Then his friend leaves our hut, pulling Mother. He has a problem: he can't help Les look for me without letting go of Mother, who kicks and bites. He has his radio in one hand, Mother in the other. He shouts at Mother and the radio. I think he is wanting a man to come from the van. Les goes in the next hut. His friend waits on the path, dodging Mother's fists.

In a minute comes a man from the van. That is a poem, I think: *a man from the van*. He's bringed a dog. I don't like dogs. The two men go into our hut, one dragging a dog, one dragging a woman. I wonder, Why is the dog? Not for little walkies, I think.

Time to leave my bin. To my right, one hundred metres away, is a few trees. No sign of Les, so I scramble out and start to run. I never have ran so fast since the boys chased me to PC Willoughby's gate. Every step I expect to hear that *Oi!* But it does not come. As I reach the trees and turn, the dog comes out dragging the man, who has my yesterday knickers in his fist. The dog sniffs the knickers, sniffs the path and pulls the man towards the wheelie bins, so I am glad to not be in the knickers or the bin.

I can't stay here though – the dog will follow my trail. I look around. Everywhere is open field. I must keep these trees between me and the policemen when I run, though it will not take me to the ruins. I am about to go off when I notice that the dog is not on my trail. It has barked at my bin, the policeman has looked but I am not inside, and now it doesn't know what to do. I realize that the rubbish stink has destroyed my scent. I am puffed, so I stay where I am to see what will happen.

It is funny. The man shouts at the dog, shoves my knickers in its face, jerks the lead. The dog lowers its nose and starts to follow the only scent it has: the one leading back to the hut. The man nearly jerks its head off, shouts *Damn useless mutt*, and treats it to a kick in the ribs. But it is not the dog's fault if the rubbish smells stronger than me. And all the time the first policeman is standing near our hut, with one eye on the search and the other on my mother's flailing fists.

I think they will notice the trees and investigate, but they do not. They stand together for a minute talking, then the one holding Mother looks at his watch and says something that starts her wailing. It makes me cry, the way she is turning her head this way and that, calling my name. I almost come out – it is the hardest thing I have ever done, not to give myself up. I want to run to her, feel her arms go round me, but no: if I go with her we will never come back. If I stay . . .

Mr Shofiq appears, shouting and waving his arms. The policemen take no notice of him but start to move away, towards the gate. My mother is screaming, struggling. A small crowd has gathered; it watches helplessly the cruel thing that is being done. I catch a glimpse of my mother as she is pulled round the corner of the hut. The spectators follow. I listen to the voices going away: Mother, Mr Shofiq, the dog. Then there is only the wind in the treetops. I am alone.

- Sixty-seven
Ruby Tanya

She's gone, your friend, said the man at the gates.

Gone? It was seven o'clock Tuesday. What d'you mean, gone?

He shrugged. Gone. Her parents are on a plane. Asra is not. She ran away.

She *did?* Too late, I realized I'd sounded delighted.

He narrowed his eyes. Yes, she did. You know nothing of this, of course?

N-no. No, I don't. You don't happen to know where . . . ?

He shook his head. How would I know? The police asked everybody here, nobody knew. Who knows the mind of a child?

Yeah, well. I took off my glasses, cleared the lenses of drizzle with my hanky, put them back on and blinked at him. Right. I better go then. Thanks. I'll see you.

I pedalled towards the village, telling myself I could have been a bit more convincing. I should have burst into tears. He was bound to wonder why I wasn't upset, my best friend gone. And why did I say, *I'll see you*? Where the heck was I going to see the guy?

In the village I hung a right onto Glebe Lane, another onto Long Lane. Long Lane's a swine on a bike in the dark, all potholes and puddles, but it was better than last time, hoofing it with a rucksack full of bedding. My heart was thumping, but not with the exercise. I'd always wanted a real adventure and now I'd got one. Me and Asra, two kids against the world.

I propped the bike against an elder near Mushroom Gap. I wasn't worried about it getting pinched: anybody daft enough to be out here on a wet Tuesday night would be too daft to know which end of a bike's the front. I couldn't see the ruins, but I knew the way all right. I set off, wading through long wet grass.

I missed the old harrow or whatever it was, but it didn't matter because the drizzle stopped and the moon came out and shone on all the wet roofs of the ruins. I scanned the upstairs windows, but Asra wasn't watching from her chair. For the first time it occurred to me she might not be here. I crept forward, wishing I had a torch. In the shadowy yard I hissed, Asra?

Ruby Tanya? She left the porch doorway, ran to me. We hugged, standing in the mud. Oh, Ruby Tanya, I am glad you have come. I have been here hours and hours, crying.

Crying?

Yes, of course. Mother and Father are in the sky; every hour they have gone another five hundred miles away from me.

I gave her a squeeze. How absolutely awful, I can't even imagine. I know I'd bawl my eyes out.

We went inside. Asra had draped a blanket over the ancient chest. We sat down. Asra bent and switched on

Gran's handy lantern, which stood on the floor and shed a comfortable halo of light. I noticed another blanket over the windows behind us, indicated it with a jerk of my head. Thought of everything, haven't you?

She shrugged. In my country, sometimes it is best that nobody knows you are home. Her voice broke up, she put her hands over her face and I knew she was thinking about her parents. I twisted sideways, put both my arms round her and held her while she wept.

My alien kid *is* home, Dad; they *all* are.

- Sixty-eight
Ruby Tanya

I hated leaving her by herself in that spooky place, but I couldn't stay all night. We'd nibbled some of Gran's chocolate, sipped water, talked a bit. She'd stopped crying, though I imagined she'd start again after I left.

The worst thing was the cold. I'd only been here an hour and a half and I was chilled to the bone. We thought she had everything she'd need, but she didn't. I looked at her, huddled in one of Gran's blankets. 'What you need is one of those little camping stoves with a gas bottle,' I said.

She shook her head. I'm all right, Ruby Tanya. This chest will be my bed. When I am in it with all these blankets I will be snug as a bug in a rug.

You're going to *sleep* in it? I shivered. *I* couldn't, it's too much like a coffin. As soon as I said this I wished I hadn't, but Asra just laughed. I will leave the lid up, she said, and let the lantern burn till morning. I think so I'll be fine.

So I left her. A cold wind had swept the clouds from the sky; the yard was awash with moonlight. I watched for a moment from the shadow of an outhouse, but nothing moved on the field. I turned. Asra had taken down the blanket and was watching me through the window, a silhouette in a frame. She raised a hand. I responded and left the yard quickly, knowing if I lingered I'd run to her.

The bike was where I'd left it. I mounted and pedalled as fast as I could to get warm, swerving round a hundred moony puddles. I wasn't going straight home; there were a couple of things I wanted to talk to Gran about.

When you've sat in a freezing ruin with nothing but cold water to sip, even green tea tastes good. I huddled over the fire, my hands wrapped round the mug, and grinned at Gran through the fragrant steam. Well, Gran. She's done it.

Who's done what to whom, sweetheart?

Asra's done a runner. They took her folks this morning.

Pigs. She looked at me. Your friend's at the old farm?

Yes, I've just come from there.

Is she OK?

I shrugged. Upset, you know, about her mum and dad. But not scared of the place like I'd be.

Does she need anything, Ruby? Apart from her mother, I mean.

I nodded. It's freezing cold, Gran. She could do with something to boil water on, brew tea. I was wondering about one of those camping stoves.

Gran smiled. I used to have one of those; might still have it somewhere. Loft, if anywhere. Now *why* didn't I think of that when I was packing the rucksack?

You gave us loads of gear, Gran. We'd've been stuffed without you.

Yes, but still, I ought to have thought. It's December tomorrow, the poor kid must be perished. She looked at me. Call in after school, Ruby. If it's in the loft I'll have it ready for

172

you, but it'll need a bottle so I might have to go to Danmouth. And if I can't find it, I'll buy another and damn the expense.

She's a treasure, my gran. I hated to ask another favour straight away, but I had to. Gran?

Yes, lovey?

Another thing she needs is a bit of company. Would you lie for me?

Gran pulled a face. Depends. Lie to whom, about what?

Would you tell Mum and Dad I was sleeping over with you when I wasn't?

Depends where you'd *actually* be sleeping, young woman.

At the farm, of course. One weekend.

She nodded. In that case, no prob. There are bad lies and good lies, and this is definitely one of the good ones.

I smiled. What'd be a bad one then, Gran?

A bad lie is one that's designed to do harm, Ruby. A *malicious* lie. The tabloids print 'em every day.

We talked till ten, then Gran phoned Mum to say I was on my way. She didn't say I'd been with her all evening, and she didn't say I hadn't. She saw to it I got no earache for being out till ten past ten, that's all.

No lie, no hassle, no harm.

- Sixty-nine
Ruby Tanya

Wednesday I was summoned to Ramsden's office in mid lesson. Not that it mattered – I was too busy thinking about the great adventure to learn anything. There was a guy with Ramsden, youngish feller with steel-rimmed specs and a grey suit. Ramsden introduced us but I don't remember what he was exactly: some sort of policeman. His name was Kershaw.

Now, Ruby Tanya, said Ramsden, I'm popping out for a few minutes. Mr Kershaw has a few questions to ask you, and I want you to help him all you can. All right?

Yes, sir.

When he'd gone, Kershaw sat down in the swivel chair and invited me to sit on the plain one meant for visitors. He smiled at me across the cluttered desk. It's Ruby Tanya Redwood, is it?

Yes.

And you're twelve years old?

Yes.

And like all twelve-year-olds you've got a best friend, haven't you, Ruby Tanya?

Yes.

And her name is Asra Saber?

Yes.

He leaned forward, rested his elbows on the desk, steepled his fingers, landed his chin on their tips and stared at me. The thick glasses made his pale eyes look big. Would you say you and Asra were very good friends? By that I mean, do you confide in each other, tell each other your most intimate secrets?

I think we do, yes. Only . . .

Only *what*, Ruby Tanya?

Well, you see, I've *lost* her, Mr Kershaw. She ran away.

Yes. He nodded. I know she ran away. What I *don't* know, and what I hope you are going to tell me, is where she is now.

I shook my head. I can't tell you, because I don't know.

He arched his brow. But you said you *confided* in each other. Surely she told you the family was being repatriated?

Oh yes, but she didn't say she was thinking of running away.

Hmm. He sat back, clasped his hands behind his neck and gazed at something in the air above my head. My halo, perhaps. Do you know what happens to those who obstruct the police in the execution of their duty, Ruby Tanya?

No, and I'm not obstructing. I don't know where she is. I wish I did.

You'd tell me, would you?

No.

He looked put out, spoke softly. Obstructing the police in the execution of their duty is an offence, Ruby Tanya. A serious offence. I've known people be sent to prison for, oh – *months*. He pulled a face. Of course, I'm talking about adults. People your age don't go to prison; they go to what's called a Juvenile Offenders' Facility. He smiled. Doesn't sound bad, does it? Well, it is. It's a place where you're yelled at and chased around from the minute you get out of your hard, narrow bed in a morning till you fall into it, exhausted, last thing at night. A place where you'll eat cold slop with hairs in it and be bullied by kids twice your size. He shook his head again. You wouldn't last a week, Ruby Tanya Redwood. Now, are you absolutely *sure* you can't help me?

I was really really scared, but I didn't tell. I couldn't. And I don't think my lie was malicious; it couldn't harm anybody except myself. I told it so my friend wouldn't be sent away to be blown up or shot. How malicious is that?

- Seventy
Asra

I wake up again and look at my watch. It is morning, seven o'clock, though it is still dark. Six hours have gone since I switched off the lantern. I am sleeping all this time. Six hours, five hundred miles an hour is three thousand miles. Mother and Father are in our country now.

But I will not weep again – there are things to do. I must get up, dress, have something for breakfast. Then I must put all of my things inside the chest so if anybody comes, it will look like nobody here.

First I need the lavatory. In the house is no bathroom. I take the lantern to the yard. All round the yard is buildings, low like the huts but of stone. I go from one to another, pushing broken doors, shining my light on machinery, sacks and straw. In one is coal. I find the lavatory in the last one. It is very disgusting and will not flush, but I don't care.

In the kitchen is a sink with a tap, but no water comes out. To wash I pour bottled water over my hands and rub my

177

face. Not a good wash, and too much drinking water gone. When it comes light I will look for water.

I am cold, even in all of my clothes. Breakfast is pressed dates, biscuits and water. Just now my people are walking to the mess for porridge and toast, scalding tea. If I was with them I would even eat some porridge.

When I have eaten and hidden all my things, I go upstairs. It is coming light. I sit on my chair and look to the hut roofs in the distance. Nobody is on the airfield, because no mushrooms in December. Soon I hear a noise like a motorbike and see a brilliant star coming across the sky. It is very strange till it flies closer, then I see what is happening. A silver helicopter is catching the rays of the sun, which has risen up there but not down here. It is beautiful to see, but I wonder if maybe it is looking for me. I leave the window and listen to it pass over. It flies on and I sit down again, waiting for the sun.

Here's a funny thing: the sun comes up, but its light comes *down*. It is true. First it touches the very tops of the trees I hid under yesterday – the thinnest twigs. Slowly, slowly it slides down each twig till it reaches the branches, then creeps down them to the trunks. It's like somebody is pouring golden syrup to see it trickle down. When it reaches the trunks it is touching the hut roofs too.

I watch till it falls on the grass. A splinter finds my window and lays a slanting ribbon down the wallpaper. I shift the chair so it falls on me but it doesn't warm me much. I look down into the muddy yard and see how the outbuildings will prevent the sun from ever falling there, at least in winter. I'm about to look away when I notice something. Beside the lavatory door a thin grey pipe sticks out of the ground. It is less than a metre high, clamped to the wall by two brackets. At the top is a small brass tap.

Water? As I stand up to go and investigate, my eye is drawn to movement on the airfield. Three men are coming this way. One is Cave-Troll Cleaver.

- Seventy-one
Asra

If only I seen the men sooner I would have ran outside, hidden in the long grass till they went away. But they are coming in the yard already. There is only one thing to do. In the wall beside the chimney breast is a tall yellow door. Through the door is a cupboard – I think so it was a wardrobe. I have looked inside: there is nothing. I put myself away and shut the door.

I am listening hard, but nobody is coming in the kitchen. In the wardrobe is very dark. I open the door a bit. I dare not come out though. I wait and listen. Still nobody comes. I get more braver, creep out, go to the room door. From here I can see the stairs. There is nobody, and no sound from the kitchen. I tiptoe to my window, not too close, and peep to the yard. The men are down there. Cave-Troll Cleaver is closing the door of an outhouse; the other two are watching him. The bags they were carrying have gone.

I watch, ready to run to the wardrobe if they are coming to the house, but they don't. One opens his pants and does a pee on the outhouse wall, which make his friends laugh very much. Then they leave the yard. I sit on the chair and watch. I think so they are heading to Mushroom Gap. I will go down to the yard and look at the tap, also at the outhouse where the men have put the bags, but not yet. Not till I know Cave-Troll Cleaver is far away.

I better not see you *though, Miss Saber,* he told to me in Mayfields, and I hope so he won't. I fear him more than any man in England.

- Seventy-two
Ruby Tanya

Mr Kershaw seemed displeased, said Ramsden when he got back from showing the policeman out. Were you not able to help, Ruby Tanya?

I couldn't answer his question, sir, I replied.

I see. Pity. Still, if you couldn't you couldn't. Off you go.

I reckon the head knew. Knew I knew where Asra was, I mean. That's why he didn't grill me himself. As a head teacher he couldn't openly show sympathy for a fugitive from the law, but I think in his heart he was on our side. I'd go so far as to say I *know* he was.

I spent the rest of the day wondering what Asra was doing. At least the sun was out – she might not be too cold. I was glad when half-three rolled round though, and I could get off to Gran's. And I was even gladder when I got there, because she'd found her old stove *and* bussed it to Danmouth for gas bottles.

I bought five, she said. One always seemed to last me an age, but I only used 'em for half an hour in the morning and half an hour at night. Your friend'll need 'em more than that.

I didn't hang about, didn't want Mum to know I'd called anywhere. I crammed the stove and gas bottles in my Adidas bag and rode home, wobbling a bit with the weight. I left bag and bike in the garage.

Hi, Mum. She was blending veg for soup. Is it all right if I take my homework round to Millie's after tea? I hadn't cleared this alibi with Millie. I hoped Mum wouldn't check.

I expect so, Ruby Tanya. She looked at me. You won't stay till ten though, will you?

I shook my head. No chance, her mum'd have a cow.

Have a *cow*? She rinsed off the blender under the tap. What on earth does that mean, young woman?

I shrugged. Dunno, Mum. Bart Simpson says it.

Ah, Bart *Simpson*. Mum hates *The Simpsons*, says it's dumb, but that's because she's never really listened to the dialogue. You've got to listen.

Dad came home in a foul mood, chuntering about vandals having no respect for other people's property. Turned out somebody had torn down the banner he'd strung across the Danmouth Road and set fire to it. Driving home he'd noticed it wasn't there, pulled over and found the charred remains in the ditch.

I was glad. I wasn't daft enough to say so, but Mum's a bit of a kamikaze lately and waded in. What d'you *expect*, Ed? she asked. Did you really think those people were going to let their children suffer that offensive message every morning on their way to school?

He went mental of course. Alien vandals was only *one* of the forces ranged against him, he told the whole street. He'd a disloyal wife to contend with as well, and a subversive daughter, and a local police force that backed invaders against the locals. He was taking a stand here, a patriotic

183

stand for Queen and country, and fat lot of thanks he was getting for it.

He stormed up to his office and slammed the door, which was good in a way because it saved me getting his OK to go out. I dried the dishes for Mum, collected my bike and bag and took the golden road to Mushroom Gap.

- Seventy-three
Asra

The tap will not turn. It is crusted with hard green stuff. I need something to bash it with. I look round the yard and find nothing. I go to the gateway to look out – I am thinking the men will return. Nobody is there, but the wall has loose stones. I pull a lump out to bash the tap with. I am not hopeful, but it works. Some of the green stuff crumbles off, and when I twist the tap it moves. A thread of water appears. When I turn the tap as far as it will go, the thread becomes a rope that splashes into the mud and spatters my jeans.

I make the palm of my hand into a cup, stick it under the tap and lift it to my mouth. The water tastes of metal, but it is a clean taste. I am very happy; now I can wash properly and drink all I want. I can rinse clothes too, but I don't know how I'll get them dry. A line of washing is not so good if police is looking for you.

I turn off the tap and have another look in the gateway. Nobody. Now I will open the door Cave-Troll Cleaver closed. Early this morning there were just some lumpy, half-rotten sacks and a heap of straw. It looks the same now, but some-where must be three bags. I glance to the gateway, then hurry inside the outhouse.

The sacks are in a line against one wall. The light is not good and the place stinks. I open the top of a sack. It is full of slimy black lumps that were potatoes long ago. I leave the sacks and walk on the straw, feeling with my feet. Straight away I find a bag. I don't feel for the other two, but carry this one to the doorway. It is very heavy. After another glance to the gateway I squat and open the zip.

I don't understand. The bag has bricks of plasticine wrapped in polythene – the same stuff we have in the craft area cupboard at school, except this is all the one yellowish colour. I don't think so Cave-Troll Cleaver is making little models out of plasticine. And I doubt it is for his children: if Cave-Troll has children he will eat them, I think.

I don't stay long wondering. Ruby Tanya will come tonight, I will ask her what she thinks. I zip up the bag, bury it in the straw and wrestle the door shut. I hope I am leaving it just as Cleaver left it.

I know what I will do now. I will use an empty mineral water bottle to carry water from the tap to the sink in the kitchen. It will take lots of trips to fill the sink, but it will pass the time and keep me warm. And of course I will go many times to the gateway.

– Seventy-four
Ruby Tanya

She was waiting in the porch with a blanket round her shoulders like a little old lady in a shawl.

I've got it, I cried, patting the bag. We'll have some tea if there's enough water.

She laughed. I think so there's enough, Ruby Tanya. She told me about the tap.

I got the stove lit. There were two pans with it, shallow oblongs that stacked and had foldaway handles. Asra filled one at the sink and put it on. We sat on the chest and watched the strong blue flame, listened to its hiss. I had three visitors, said Asra.

What? I gasped.

She smiled. Don't worry, they didn't know they were visiting me.

She told me about Cleaver and his friends, the bags in the outhouse, plasticine.

Plasticine? I frowned. Are you *sure* that's what it is, Asra?

187

She pulled a face. A *bit* sure, she said. D'you want to look?

I shook my head. Suppose they came to collect while we were snooping?

Oooh, *don't*! She shivered. Cave-Troll Cleaver in the dark: I think so police is better.

I wondered how Cleaver and his mates knew the ruins existed, and decided Dad probably told them. He's an estate agent after all; he'd know about empty properties on his patch. *In need of slight attention,* he'd say if he was selling this one.

I'd looked forward to this, sipping and yarning over the stove like swagmen round a campfire. I'd imagined the two of us relaxed, Asra warm for once, enjoying each other's company, the real world far away in the dark. Now she'd told me about the visitors I felt jumpy, vulnerable, far from help. I kept getting up, lifting a corner of the blanket, peering out. All I saw was my own face and the reflected glow from the stove, but it didn't stop me doing it. I was unhappy at the thought of leaving Asra here at night. I had to mention it.

Asra, why don't you come and sleep at Gran's? I don't like the idea of you being here by yourself, now that horrible man's been.

Asra smiled, shook her head. I'm fine, Ruby Tanya, honestly. He doesn't know anyone's here, he didn't come in the house, and I don't think so he'll come at night. I'll be very careful.

I couldn't budge her. She was chuffed with the stove, the water supply she'd found. She mentioned washing. I said I'd take it to Gran's. I promised to bring tins of beans tomorrow; other tins as well. I made her promise to keep a careful look-out, especially when fetching water or going to the loo. I left at half eight, with bits of her laundry in my bag to drop off at Gran's.

Biking down Long Lane under the moon, I thought about the men's visit to the ruins. Why would a bunch of dodgy guys carry stuff right out there and hide it in an outhouse? I could've understood if the bags were crammed with dosh or loot of some sort, but *plasticine*? What was in the other bags, and would Asra be tempted to take a peek in the morning? I hoped not.

Gran took the bits and bobs of washing, no sweat. She gave me beans and tomatoes in tins, and a packet of dried pasta. I didn't tell her about Cleaver and his mates, the plasticine. No point worrying her.

Get it all done, sweetheart? goes Mum when I walk in. For a second I think she's sussed everything, but she means homework.

Yes, thanks, I said. Where's Dad?

Upstairs doing *his* homework.

Huh?

Practising his speech for Monday.

Oh, right.

That night I had the weirdest dream. I was queuing to get into one of the outhouses at the ruins. That was where Dad was due to speak. There were hundreds of people in the muddy yard. Cave-Troll Cleaver was on the door. Before he'd let you in, you had to stick your feet under a running tap and wash the mud off your shoes. It was taking ages but nobody minded, they were all laughing and joking. The outhouse was fifty times bigger inside than outside, like the Tardis. There were no seats, you stood on straw. On the platform, three men sat behind a long table. One of them was Cleaver, even though he was on the door. When it was time, the place went dark, like the lights going down at the pictures. Only the platform was bright. We all went quiet, but instead of Dad appearing the three guys started singing, swaying from side to side in time with the music. What they sang was, *Yes, sir, yes, sir, three bags full.* Just the one line, over and over. A few people in the audience started to join in, and soon we were all singing our hearts out, clapping to the beat. At this point, a Union Jack the size of a football pitch came drifting down from somewhere above and settled on us, pressing everybody to their knees. It was hot and heavy in the folds of the flag, impossible to breathe. I kicked and writhed but there was no way out, I was suffocating.

I woke gasping, flinging back the duvet. There was a smell like plasticine. It was ages before I got back to sleep.

- Seventy-five
Ruby Tanya

Thursday breakfast Mum asks, Is there something you'd like to tell me, Ruby Tanya? Dad had left for work, thank goodness.

I played dumb. What sort of something, Mum? I knew what was bothering her, she's not daft.

Your friend Asra. I just wonder if you know more than you're telling.

I don't know what you mean.

Mum sighed. I care about Asra too, sweetheart, but have you thought about her parents, what it must be doing to them, knowing their daughter's missing in a strange land a thousand miles away?

I shrugged. They didn't want her to live in their country, Mum, and she isn't.

No, but you see, they don't even know she's alive. A child of twelve, wandering the countryside. Anything might happen. A killer, for instance. They'll be imagining all sorts of dreadful things. I know *I* would be.

I must admit I hadn't thought of that. Couldn't tell Mum though, could I? In fact I didn't know *what* to say. She gave me a moment, then said, If *I* had a friend in Asra's position, I think I'd try getting a message to her mum and dad. Not sure how – I don't suppose they're on the internet. I might try a local paper: they'd find a way, I'm sure. Anyway – her tone became brisk – this won't get the baby bathed. She stood up, started stacking plates. There's no baby, it's just her way of saying, time to get on, things to do.

I was puzzled. One minute she seemed about to interrogate me, really push it, and the next she's dropped the subject in favour of washing up. She spoke with her back to me. Your father seems to be coming to his senses, by the way.

How d'you mean?

He's decided to drop those new pals of his, Feltwell and Cleaver.

Hey, I smiled. Does that mean he'll stop picking on the people up the camp?

She shook her head. 'Fraid not, sweetheart. When I say *coming to his senses*, I don't mean he's going to be *sensible*. Bridge too far, that'd be. No, he'll go ahead, but without any more help from Feltwell and Co. I'm relieved: they seem a sinister bunch to me.

And me, I nodded. Especially that Cleaver. Cave-Troll, they call him, Asra's scared stiff of . . .

Yes, well. She didn't turn to see my blush. If I had a friend like Asra, I think I'd suggest she might be safer giving herself up than remaining at large with creatures like him prowling about. She slotted a plate in the rack. *If* I knew where she was, I mean.

- Seventy-six
Asra

I am not so tired Thursday morning. I left the stove on low all night; it kept me warm a bit and was company. I take down the blanket and look out at the yard. It has been frosty.

I have hot tea for breakfast, and toast. Is not so good the toast: my stove is not a toaster. I wish I would carry in some coal from the outhouse and make a fire, but I daren't make the chimney smoke. What if somebody seen it? Instead I get six flat stones out of the wall and stack them under the sink. I put the stove on top of the stones. In the sink is water. I hope so the stove will warm the water. While it is doing this I go out to the toilet. Then, I don't know why, I go look at those bags again. I must be crazy.

I find one in the straw, take it to the doorway and unzip it. I hope so it is another bag but it is the one I look in yesterday. I take out a slab of the plasticine to sniff, then I hear a man coughing. He is not in the yard but will be soon. I zip up the bag, push it in the straw and run out. The door is hard to close, I don't think so I do it right. The cough is very close now. I run in the house.

Cleaver comes in the yard, enjoying a cigarette that is making him cough. I am in the porch, ready to run upstairs if he comes this way, but it will be no use. He will see my stuff, the stove under the sink. He will find me in the wardrobe. Eat me.

He does not come. I can't believe he is so not curious. If *I* see a ruined house I must explore. He's brought another bag for the outhouse. He even does not notice the door is different. *Cleaver* is close to *clever* but not close enough, Allah be praised. He puts the bag in the outhouse, pushes the door shut and leans on the wall to finish his cigarette. I wish the cigarette will finish him instead.

I dare not move, try not to breathe. He sucks in smoke and lets it out slowly, looking at the house. Any second something will catch his eye, make him want a closer look. It doesn't happen, just suck, suck, suck. Each suck is making the cigarette shorter. Now and then he removes it from his lips to cough. Once he makes a choking, roaring noise like a dinosaur and spits a big, green gob in the mud. At last, when my nerves are screaming and I am bursting to scream myself, he throws down the butt and shambles off without a backward glance. I think so I have nine lives, like a cat.

When Cleaver has left the yard I find I've got the slab of plasticine in my hand.

- Seventy-seven
Ruby Tanya

Dad didn't drive straight to his office in Danmouth that Thursday morning. He called in at PC Willoughby's house first, to tell the policeman what he'd seen and heard at the BF rally last Sunday. He hadn't told Mum he was going to do this, and we didn't find out about it till after, when it had nearly cost him his life.

By sheer rotten luck, Dad came out of the police house just as Cave-Troll Cleaver was driving along Aspen Arbour on his way to Long Lane and the ruins. Cleaver clocked him, and mentioned it when he phoned his boss later. Sefton Feltwell couldn't possibly know *why* Dad had been to the police but that didn't matter: his fate was sealed.

Anyway, we didn't know any of this at the time. I biked off to school as usual, and Mum went to her work at the charity shop. Normal lessons had more or less ground to a halt because of the Christmas concert. There were rehearsals of *Joseph* morning and afternoon, and as if *this* didn't make school feel unreal enough, we found ourselves suddenly famous.

FEARS GROW FOR VANISHED SCHOOLGIRL was the headline in one tabloid. Normally you wouldn't find a newspaper anywhere near school, except the odd racing sheet in the staffroom, but now kids were bringing them from home and swapping them in the yard. Our village had become this week's focus for the paedophile hysteria industry. The school was mentioned loads of times, and Ramsden warned us not to talk to reporters. Apparently a few had been spotted on a sponsored sensation sniff around the village. Tipton Lacey seemed set to take over from Bradford as the capital of deviance, crime and racial strife.

Made things twice as scary for me, I can tell you. It felt like the eyes of the whole country were on me, when all I was trying to do was help my friend. People were saying Asra had been murdered or abducted. I was amazed the police hadn't searched the ruins; they must've assumed she'd left the district. I was thankful, of course, but I knew they were bound to get round to it before long. I wondered how many years I'd get when they found her – found out I was behind it all – and whether a tabloid might pay a million pounds for my story. I came *this* close to betraying my best friend.

I didn't know it then, but events were soon to take matters out of my hands and leave me and Asra at the mercy of the man we feared the most.

– Seventy-eight
Ruby Tanya

I bet *you* know where she is, said Millie at afternoon break. I nearly fainted. Then I saw she was grinning.

Oh yeah, I managed to joke. It's a scam we dreamed up: baffle the police, the immigration people and everybody else, then come out to one of the tabloids. The paper gives us a million to show 'em how we did it, they run the story with pictures and everything, and me and Asra split the dosh and sit in Mayfields getting fat.

I didn't want Millie around really. I was thinking about what Mum had said at breakfast. *If I had a friend in Asra's position, I think I'd try getting a message to her mum and dad.* She'd said other stuff as well; it was almost as if she knew. She's not daft – it wouldn't surprise me if she'd put two and two together and realized. Or maybe Gran had had a word. What *would* surprise me would be if she knew and didn't try to stop it.

I might try a local paper. What was that if it wasn't a message, a bit of advice? All right, so why not call the *Star*?

I would withhold my number; they wouldn't know who called.

I had the number – I'd entered every one I could think of when I first got the phone. I told Millie I had to pee, hurried to the cloakroom. Locked in a cubicle, I sat on the seat and thumbed in the number.

Tipton Lacey Star, Tracey speaking, how may I help you?

It's about the missing girl.

May I have your name, caller?

No name. Put me through to someone, it's urgent.

One moment, I'll try the newsroom.

Hello, newsroom.

Oh, hi. It's about the missing girl.

Asra Saber. What about her?

She's safe and well.

Who *is* this, please? How d'you know she's safe and well?

I can't give my name, but I know. We're in contact.

Will you tell me where she is, love?

No.

Then why call the *Star*? What d'you want us to do?

Get the message to Asra's parents.

What message?

That she's safe and well of course. They must be frantic.

Yes, but they're abroad. I'm not sure we'd be able . . .

Try, right? I've got to go. 'Bye.

Did I do the right thing, or would the call enable them to trace me somehow? I'd no way of knowing, I could only wait. I lurked in my cubicle till the buzzer went, then hurried to my next class hoping Asra'd be pleased when I told her. Hoping I'd be free to go to her tonight.

- Seventy-nine
Ruby Tanya

Homework at Millie's again, I suppose? said Mum at tea time. If she hasn't sussed everything I'm Posh Beckham.

Leave her alone, defended Dad. Better she spends her time with Millie than with some terrorist's kid from that camp.

It might sound like my parents were fighting again, but they weren't. Dad had just told Mum he'd talked to the police, so she was fairly happy. Not as happy as if he'd said he was joining an asylum seekers' support group, but still.

Yes, I said. History and RE. Her mum's getting us a pizza after. This was only partly a lie: *I* was getting a pizza for Asra.

Now *that's* what I call a friend, smarmed Dad.

It had turned colder. The ruts and puddles of Long Lane had ice on them. If it hadn't been for that hot pizza inside my jacket I'd have frozen to death. Asra was pleased to see us both. We huddled close to the stove while she demolished the pizza. Between bites, she told me about Cleaver.

Hell's *bells*, Asra, I gasped, you want to stay right away from that outhouse. What if he hadn't coughed?

She nodded. I know, I won't go in it again. I got a bit of his plasticine.

Did you? Where is it?

It is in my bestest room, in the wardrobe. I'll show you after.

She didn't though, because when she'd finished eating I told her about my call to the *Star*. It pleased her even more than the pizza. Her eyes shone. Oh, Ruby Tanya, I hope, hope, *hope*, they get a message to Mother and Father. I worry about them all the time, worrying about me. Thank you for thinking of it, you are *so* clever.

Not me, I admitted. It was Mum's idea.

Your *mum*? But that must mean she . . .

Knows. I nodded. I think she does, Asra. The amazing thing is, she seems to be going along with it; even gave me an alibi for tonight.

That is wonderful, Ruby Tanya, but what about your father?

Oh, he'll never change. He definitely doesn't suspect though, and Mum won't tell him.

Are you sure?

Absolutely sure.

I had another go at her about staying with my gran. It's got a lot colder, I said. What if the gas runs out? You'll freeze.

It's still the first can, she told me, and I've had it on ever such a lot. It won't run out for ages. She grinned. I even washed in warm water.

Yeah? I smiled. Oh well, if it's getting *that* comfy I think I'll join you for a night or two. How about tomorrow?

She thought I was joking, I knew she would. When I told

200

her Gran had agreed to lie for me, that I'd be sleeping over Friday and Saturday she was chuffed to little mint balls. I can't *wait*, she squealed, hugging me.

You'll have to, I told her. There's a little feather bed waiting for me.

It was a numbing ride home without the pizza. History go all right? enquired Dad as I hung up my jacket.

I nodded. Fine thanks.

RE?

Fine too. Where's Mum?

Over at your gran's.

At *Gran's*? Why?

Don't ask me. Your gran phoned, your mum went to see her. Go get ready for bed, love: school tomorrow.

I sat on my bed and gazed through the window at the lights. Mum and Gran. Gran and Mum. I thought I knew exactly what they were talking about and I was right, though I didn't find out for sure till after.

- Eighty
Ruby Tanya

The *Star* prints readers' letters. That Friday morning there was one by Gran, and it had inspired an editorial. Both were about Asra, and they spoiled Dad's breakfast. He flicked through, groaned and slid the paper across to Mum, who read the two items and passed it to me without comment.

Gran had written about the cruelty of sending parents out of the country while their child was missing. She invited village parents to try to imagine how they would feel if they had to fly home at the end of a holiday, leaving their child wandering somewhere in Spain, hunted like a criminal.

I thought it was a great letter. The editor obviously agreed with me, because the piece he'd written supported Gran's point all along the line. If Asra Saber was a village child, he said, our hearts would go out to her parents and we'd all be helping in the search.

I wasn't crazy about that last bit, mind: *helping in the search*. There were more than enough people looking for Asra already, but it felt like the editor was on our side. Well, not on our *side* exactly. I was pretty sure he wouldn't approve of the way me and Asra had gone about things, but he and his paper were certainly against those who were against us, if you know what I mean.

This was the morning I had to ask Mum if I could sleep over tonight and tomorrow at Gran's. I'd been dreading it before, but not as much as now. They'd talked together last night. What if Gran told Mum about the alibi I'd asked her to provide? The two of them might have decided it was a bad idea for me to sleep over at the ruins. Knowing I was going to ask, Mum'd be ready with a straight no. What of my promise to Asra then?

It felt like ages till Dad went off to work. As the Volvo crunched along the drive I screwed up my courage. Mum?

What is it, sweetheart?

I was wondering, would it be all right if I stayed at Gran's this weekend? I mentioned it to her, and she seemed . . .

Mum nodded. Gran told me, Ruby Tanya. Of *course* it's all right. She smiled. When we love someone, we don't like to think of them being all alone, do we? Too sad.

Th-thanks, Mum. I'll go pack a few things then. I left the room quickly, blushing.

Take a woolly, sweetheart, she called after me. It's sure to be colder than you think. And give me a ring so I'll know you're all right.

Colder than you think? Gran's cottage is too cosy if anything, and I'm always all right there.

But she's not talking about Gran's, is she?

- Eighty-one
Asra

A terrible thing has happened and I don't know what to do. This morning I am using the dirty old lavatory when I hear people in the yard. Cleaver is one, I know his voice. I am very scared. What if they go in the house, or if one of them decides to come in here? What if they notice my many foot-prints to and fro? I move silently, making myself ready. If the door opens I will burst out – they might be surprised enough so I can get away. Not so good, but no other way.

I listen. They are putting more things in the outhouse. I pray to Allah to make them go away like before. I hear the scrape of the outhouse door closing. Will they look in the house now, find my things? If they move that way I must go at once, leave everything.

They are standing in the mud, lighting cigarettes, talking. There is a hole in the lavatory door, shaped like a crescent moon. I put my eye to it. Four men in a half-circle, two metres away. I daren't even withdraw my eye. Cleaver is speaking.

Right, lads, better get back. Sefton'll be up later for a shufti. Eagle's Nest, he calls it. Sparrer's Dump, *I* call it.

The other men laugh, throwing down cigarette ends, treading them into the mud, turning away. I breathe in deeply. My prayer is answered but I wait a bit. Somewhere an engine starts up. I come out, but I am hearing Cleaver's voice in my head. *Sefton'll be up later for a shufti.*

Up *where*? Here of course, where else? And what does *later* mean? Later today, most likely. *Eagle's Nest* must be the house. I don't think so they will call a poky little outhouse Eagle's Nest. So Sefton Feltwell's coming to look at the house, which has all my stuff in it.

What can I do? I could run away of course, leave everything and just go. But where would I go? To Ruby Tanya's gran's house? *I've come to live in your house, Ruby Tanya's gran. I've lost your stove and your bedding and your towels and your pans and everything, but you don't mind, do you?* I cannot do this. The only other thing I can think of is to take everything out of the house and put it somewhere else till Sefton has had his shufti, then bring it back. But where do I take it, and who says the house will be empty when it's time to bring it back? Eagle's Nest might be occupied tonight and ever after.

There's no other way though. I must remove all trace of myself from the house. Find somewhere to stow my things, stow *myself*. And Ruby Tanya's coming tonight. I can't let her walk into the yard, can I?

Oh, Father, Mother, I don't know what to *do*.

- Eighty-two
Ruby Tanya

The day had seemed endless but finally I was on my way, wobbling up Long Lane in the dark with two supermarket bags on the handlebars. I'd called at Gran's to confirm my alibi and to pick up Asra's laundry, and she'd found her old sleeping bag in the loft. You might be glad of this, she said. She didn't say Mum knew where I'd really be this weekend and I didn't ask, but I'd a strong feeling she wouldn't need to lie for me.

I was approaching Mushroom Gap when I saw movement by the hedge. Somebody was there. I went into a U-turn that was impossibly tight. The bags made it harder and my wheels skidded sideways on the gritty surface, throwing me heavily to the ground. I shoved the bike off my leg and was scrambling to my feet when I heard my name.

Ruby Tanya, I'm sorry, are you all right?

Asra? What the heck you doing here? Did you think I wasn't coming or something? My leg was stinging like mad, grazed through my jeans.

Asra picked up the bike, leaned it on the hedge. Yes . . . no. I mean, that's not why I'm here. I knew you'd come, but I've left the ruins. We must get away before Feltwell comes.

Feltwell's coming here?

Yes, for a shufti. Cleaver said so.

A shufti at *what*, Asra?

The house. He is calling it Eagle's Nest.

But . . . all our stuff. He'll see it, know you've been living there.

No, I have moved it all.

Where *to*, for Pete's sake?

There's a . . . a shed, a barn or something, in the field behind the house. The things are there. Come, let's go away. Bring the bike.

It was hard, wheeling the bike through the long grass. The barn was twice as far as the ruins, right in the middle of a field. My leg was killing me and I had a hundred questions. As we stumbled along in the pitchy dark, Asra told me how she'd overheard Cleaver and realized she'd have to get out. But the barn's got no roof, I protested. We can't sleep there.

Asra shrugged. I think so we will sleep, she said. Tomorrow we can return to the ruins, if nobody is there.

And if somebody *is* there, then what?

I do not know, Ruby Tanya.

We were ages getting to the barn – what was left of it. Like I said, there was no roof, and an end wall had partly collapsed. She'd been busy, using lengths of rotting timber and some old bin liners to erect a flimsy shelter across a corner. She'd lined its floor with bags and piled her stuff there, leaving just enough room for the two of us to squeeze in. There, she sighed as we settled. Snug as a bug in a rug.

D'you think we could risk a light? I asked.

Oh yes, our back is to the ruins. Nothing will be seen. She switched on Gran's lantern and I glanced about me.

You *are* clever, I gasped. I could never have turned bits of rubbish into a place like this.

She pulled a face. In my country are many broken houses, from the bombing. People must have shelter. This is the shelter they have.

I shook my head. I suppose even a quarter of a hut with blankets for walls seems luxurious compared to that.

Asra nodded. Yes it does, for a little while.

She'd even thought to fill a plastic water bottle. We nibbled chocolate, sipped water and talked. This might sound crazy but I loved every minute of that long, long evening, huddled with my best friend in a broken-down barn in the middle of a field, talking by lantern-light. Our shelter might be crude but it kept the drizzle out, and the wind. We *were* snug as a bug in a rug.

And in a couple of days' time we were going to be sharing a space that'd make this seem like the penthouse suite of a five-star hotel.

- *Eighty-three*
Ruby Tanya

We *did* sleep. I suspect we were warmer snuggled together in that rough shelter than we would've been in the ruins. I'd had it in mind to spy on Feltwell, try to find out what *Eagle's Nest* meant, but when it came to it we were too comfy, too lazy to leave our snug bivouac.

Saturday morning we lay watching it get light. *Half*-light actually, because everything was shrouded in thick mist. Asra smiled. Just right, eh, Ruby Tanya? We can move our stuff back and nobody will see us.

I'd been thinking about that. I looked at her. We can't go back though, can we?

Why not?

Feltwell. He's chosen the ruins for his Eagle's Nest, whatever that means. And whatever it means, one thing's for sure: he's going to show up sooner or later with Cleaver and the rest. They're up to something, with those bags they've been hiding in the outhouse. They could move in *today*. I shook my head. We've had it as far as the ruins're concerned – have to think of somewhere else.

Asra nodded. You are right but that's OK, I can live here.

Here? I shook my head. It's all right for a night or two but you can't stay here. There's no water.

You can bring water.

What about when you want to . . . you know?

She shrugged. Bombs break lavatories, Ruby Tanya, in my country. People manage.

Yes, OK, but . . .

What?

Let's face it, Asra, it's Granny time. I hoped it wouldn't come to this, wanted us to manage by ourselves, but Feltwell's screwed it up. When there's a roof and a warm bed waiting, it doesn't make sense to—

Listen! Asra cocked her head on one side. I listened. Motors, more than one, some way off, getting closer. We kicked off the sleeping bag and scrambled to our feet. The sound was behind us, in the direction of the ruins. We left our corner and peered through a broken wall into the mist, ready to flee if necessary. The farmhouse was barely visible, a shadow on a field of pearly grey. It was cold; our breath rose in plumes round our heads.

The motors were louder now, much closer. We thought it was Feltwell, but it wasn't. A weird blue glow became visible, separating into four pulsating blobs. I gripped Asra's arm. Police! I hissed. They must be looking for you. Come on.

The cars stopped. Their fog lamps bathed the four walls of the house. Ghostly figures closed in on the yard as we left the barn and melted into the mist.

- Eighty-four
Ruby Tanya

We didn't go far, and they didn't stay long. A hawthorn shrub gave us something to hide behind, though we hardly needed it. My worry was that they'd notice the barn and come for a look. If that happened our stuff'd be lost *and* they'd know Asra wasn't far away.

They didn't come. Maybe the mist saved us. We couldn't see the barn or the ruins from our hiding place but we could hear voices, see that pulsating glow. I pictured them rooting through everything, looking for the smallest clue such as a matchstick or a hair but they couldn't have: they weren't there ten minutes.

As the motors started up Asra whispered, I wonder if they found Cleaver's bags?

I shrugged. Dunno. They'd have to move the straw. I don't think they were there long enough. We stayed close to our shrub as the cars lurched away and the blue glow dwindled to nothing. Tell you what, I murmured.

What?

They might've done us a favour.

What favour, Ruby Tanya?

Well, if Cleaver knows the police've been, maybe he'll abandon this Eagle's Nest idea, find somewhere else.

Asra shook her head. I don't think so he will know, Ruby Tanya. How will he know?

I shrugged. If he had someone watching, saw the cars go up Long Lane. I dunno, it was just a thought.

We made our way back to the barn, put a pan of water on the stove, nibbled biscuits while we waited. My feet were wet and I was frozen. I held up the plastic bottle, showed Asra the water-level. Litre at the most, I said. I daren't use Long Lane today 'cos Feltwell and his guys'll come that way, and this will all be gone by tonight. We can't stay here, Asra.

She looked at me. If we can't use Long Lane to fetch water, she said, how can we use it to get to your gran's house, with your bike and all this stuff? And don't forget the police, they could be near. At least we're safe from *them* here – they've searched.

She had me there. I shook my head, staring into the pan. You're right, we're stuck. I looked up. I could go for water *now*, before the mist goes.

She shook her head, smiling. No need, Ruby Tanya. Look. She pointed up at our binbag roof. There's water.

I stood on tiptoe to look. The roof sagged towards the middle, where there was no prop. A small puddle of rain-water had accumulated there. I looked at my friend. You're Ray Mears in disguise, aren't you? She'd never watched him so I had to explain, which spoilt it a bit.

She made me hold the other pan while she guided the rainwater into it, and we didn't lose a drop. There wasn't much but, as the old lady said when she peed in the ocean,

212

every little helps. Asra rearranged the roof so the same thing would happen next time it rained.

And so we stayed. I didn't want us to. Didn't want *her* to, Sunday night by herself and all the nights after that, but she insisted. If she hadn't, we'd have been spared a horrifying experience and half the people of Tipton Lacey would be dead.

- Eighty-five
Ruby Tanya

The mist lingered all day, which was good in a way because we didn't have to worry about being seen by anybody who might come to the farm. We used the time to sort our equipment, stowing it in an organized way so we could find things, even in the dark. I helped Asra rig an extension to the bivouac using some spare binliners and lengths of wood. We kept our ears cocked for sounds from the ruins, but we didn't hear anything. We kept our own noise down in case of sharper ears there.

It was getting dark by three o'clock. We couldn't do anything useful and we'd soon have got cold sitting around, so we retreated to our corner and got in the sleeping bag. It wasn't designed for two but me and Asra aren't big; we managed.

Once we'd put a pan of our precious water on the stove for a suppertime drink, there was nothing to do but talk. We talked and talked; it was nice. Asra told me about her country, before the bombs and the bad men. I'd always

214

thought hot countries had warm nights, but she said it was colder there at night than here. She talked about her parents, wondered what they were doing, whether the *Star* had got a message to them. I said I'd phone them Monday and ask.

We talked about my parents too, especially Dad. Turned out the asylum seekers saw him as a cunning politician, the mastermind behind their persecution. I laughed. Dad's not a *mastermind*, Asra, he's a moron. The Moron of Tipton Lacey, I call him. He should wear a jester suit, and a chain of office. A lavatory chain'd be about right.

I told her about the letter I'd found, the one from Feltwell. *He's* the mastermind, I said. He wants the airfield, and he's using my dad to help him get your people out. I think Dad's in deeper than he intended, mind: Feltwell and his gang're way out of his league. I bet he'll back off once this speech thing's over.

We discussed Feltwell, wondering why he needed an Eagle's Nest in the ruins. What was he planning? Was it to do with the airfield, or something more sinister? We didn't get anywhere, but it helped to pass the time. At eight we had our bedtime drink of cocoa and settled down for the night. I woke up once and heard rain pattering on our roof. Good, I thought dreamily, another precious puddle. Ray Mears was fast asleep so I wriggled into a new position and drifted off.

Sunday dawned clear, bright and frosty. We had to leave our corner to take our morning pees, but apart from that we kept our heads down just in case, though we'd noticed no sign of life at the farm. The rain I'd heard in the night had left a bigger puddle than yesterday's, and we used most of it to wash our faces and hands and brush our teeth.

It got a bit boring as the morning wore on. It'd have been better if we could've walked on the airfield a bit to get warm, but we couldn't assume nobody was at the farm, just because we hadn't heard anything. At eleven o'clock Asra said, You don't have to stay, you know. You could go home, have your Sunday dinner.

No way! I cried. I like being with you, you div. I'm here till dusk at least. I'll phone home though, I promised Mum.

It was a weird call.

Hi, Mum, it's me.

Ruby Tanya, I expected to hear from you yesterday.

Sorry, Mum, we got a bit busy, I forgot.

Are you all right?

Sure.

And what about your—?

She's fine too.

Good. What are the two of you up to this morning?

Oh, lazing around, you know. Sunday.

Don't blame you. Your father and I are off to the garden centre, border plants.

Wow, lucky you.

There's no need to be sarky, young woman. What time are you thinking of coming home?

Oh, half-four, five.

It'll be dark by then.

Yes, Mum, that's because it's winter.

I *know* . . . oh, all right. We'll expect you around half-four then. Give our love to . . .

I will, Mum. She sends you hers.

Thank you, darling. 'Bye.

'Bye, Mum.

Both pretending I'm at Gran's.

- Eighty-six
Ruby Tanya

It was ten to five when I got home. Dad was up in his office, practising the speech he'd deliver tomorrow at the village hall. Saved some possible hassle. Mum told me I smelled, but you can't have everything, can you? She ran me a hot bath, and I luxuriated in it for an hour and a quarter while she cooked me a meal. To avoid conversations, I pretended I needed a really early night and Mum pretended to believe me. I lay in my nice warm bed, wondering what Asra was doing, wishing she were here. I hadn't said anything to Mum about Feltwell's pals, bags in the outhouse, Eagle's Nest and all that. It would have been too awkward: she assumed I'd slept there the last two nights. I couldn't be bothered explaining about the barn. And anyway, we were still pretending I'd spent the weekend at Gran's.

Asif and Keith showed up at school Monday morning and actually *talked* to each other in the yard. Maybe we should all spend a few days lying next to one another in hospital. That was the upside. The downside was, loads of kids came

217

up to me and said their folks were off to the village hall tonight to listen to Dad. They thought I'd be pleased by the support he had in the village.

One lad asked me what BF stood for. I told him Basil Fawlty.

Ramsden had us pray for Asra's safety in assembly. Her mum and dad's safety would've been more to the point in my opinion, but there you go. At least it reminded me I was supposed to phone the *Star*.

I did it at morning break, in the toilets.

Tipton Lacey Star, Tracey speaking, how may I help you?

Oh, hi, newsroom please, it's urgent.

May I have your name, caller?

No name. I called last Thursday.

Oh yes. One moment.

Newsroom.

Oh, hi, are you the man I spoke to last week, about Asra Saber?

Ye-es.

I asked if you could get a message to her parents?

Yes, I remember.

Well *did* you?

Not personally, but I gather my editor managed something through a radio station out there, a brief message. Of course there's no guarantee they heard it.

Course not, but hey, thanks. Thanks a lot.

Could I have your name please?

No, sorry. 'Bye.

A message on radio! I couldn't wait to tell Asra, so of course the day dragged on for ever. We had rehearsals, then there were some rehearsals, and after that, just for a change, they stuck in a few rehearsals before we got down to rehearsing.

Tea time, Dad was hyper. He'd taped his speech, all of it. He kept pressing play, stop, rewind, play. Listening to this bit and that bit, over and over. We're supposed to be eating a meal and he's like, does that sound OK love?

Fine, goes mum, who's despising the whole thing. You'll have them eating out of your hand. She's being ironic but Dad doesn't notice; he's too hooked on this Councillor Redwood trip.

The upside was, he didn't object when I mentioned I was off to Millie's. If I'd said I was off to Sirius it wouldn't have got through. Mum knew exactly where I was going, of course. She wasn't happy about it, but she played along.

- Eighty-seven
Ruby Tanya

I called out softly as I approached the barn. Asra? It was one of those clear, starry evenings that promises a cold night. She was standing by the broken wall, wrapped in a blanket. We hugged.

Long day, she whispered.

I nodded. I bet. Let's get the stove going, have a brew. We headed for the bivouac. I've a bit of good news.

What? She found a matchbox, squatted at the stove.

The *Star* got a message for your parents on the radio. They'll know you're safe, Asra.

The gas ignited with a plop.

They have no radio, Ruby Tanya.

I hadn't thought of that. What a bummer. I'd pictured making her day.

She poured water into a pan and set it carefully on the stove. There is always a radio somewhere, she murmured. Perhaps somebody heard the message and told Father.

I hope so. I was arranging the sleeping bag, thought we'd get in, warm up.

Asra looked at me. Nobody came to the farm, she said. I think so I will move back if you help me.

Course I'll help, but are you *sure* nobody's there?

She shrugged. We didn't see anybody, only police. I think so police scared those bad men so they didn't come.

Fine. I smiled. At least you'll have a roof.

She nodded. And the chest to sleep in. I will be snug, but we will have tea before.

First, I corrected. We will have tea *first*.

We drank it scalding, our hands wrapped round Gran's mugs. I think we better go empty-handed first trip, I said, make sure nobody's about.

We will look *first*, grinned Asra. She's a quick learner.

We finished our tea, extinguished the flame. I put the torch in my pocket and we set off towards the starlit farm. We didn't know it, but we wouldn't be back for our stuff.

221

- Eighty-eight
Ruby Tanya

The yard was silent, full of angular shadows. The outhouse doors were closed. The farmhouse windows were black rectangles, no light behind them. Clearly the place was unoccupied.

We stood in the gateway. It's all right, isn't it? whispered Asra. Her breath drifted like smoke.

I nodded. Think so, yeah. Feels spooky though. I'll just take a peek through the window.

I crossed the yard, cupped my hands and peered into the kitchen. I wondered if the police had left evidence of their visit, but it was too dark to see anything. Asra was at my elbow. I whispered, hang on a sec, and stepped into the porch. I switched on the torch and made a quick sweep of the kitchen. My heart kicked. The chest lid was up – it seemed to be full of stuff. In a corner was a stack of inflatable mattresses, and some cardboard boxes. They've been here, I cried, and they'll be back. Let's go.

We were crossing the porch when we heard a motor. I

grabbed Asra's elbow. Come on!

No. She held back. Look! A beam of light swung down the sky and lit up the gateway like the angel appearing to the shepherds. A mouse couldn't have crossed that glare unseen. As we stood paralysed, doors slammed. The motor died but the light didn't. Two figures appeared in it, coming this way. One was Cave-Troll Cleaver.

Asra whimpered. I was still holding her elbow. I jerked it. Come on, out the back. I'd switched off the torch but there was light enough. We pelted along a passage to the back door. It was locked or bolted or something. We hadn't time to mess around, Cleaver'd be halfway across the yard.

Upstairs! cried Asra. The wardrobe. We turned, dashed across the kitchen to the stairs and up like mountain goats. We'd just crossed the bedroom floor when Cave-Troll's foot-falls sounded below. The wardrobe door had a creak on it that damn near got us caught, but the thug was talking to his mate and didn't hear. We squashed into the wardrobe and pulled the door to.

Heavy boots began to mount the stairs.

- Eighty-nine
Ruby Tanya

We daren't breathe. The thought of Cleaver wrenching open the wardrobe door melted my muscles. I almost collapsed. We listened as he clumped along the landing, looking in rooms. He must have spotted us crossing the kitchen: he knew we were up here somewhere.

The footfalls were close; he was in the doorway. Ah! He'd seen something, was coming, we felt the vibration through our feet. A second or two and he'd have us. I cowered, staring at the crack where the door didn't fit.

They're up here, he called. He was by the window. We heard a metallic scrape, a rattle as he carried something past our hiding place and stumped out to the landing. Dunno why they put 'em up here. He went downstairs grumbling to himself.

We breathed out, relaxing momentarily. Chairs, whispered Asra. I think so he was finding chairs.

I nodded in the dark. Thank goodness, but how do we get out of here now they're settling in?

Asra shrugged. We can't, Ruby Tanya. We must wait till they go. I would rather stay in this wardrobe for ever than let that man catch me.

I shook my head. Could be days, Asra. Chairs, mattresses, grub: doesn't sound like the odd half-hour, does it?

Still we must wait, she breathed.

Voices reached us from the kitchen. Seemed very close in fact, as though the guys were talking right outside the wardrobe. We could hear every word. We listened: Cleaver was speaking.

. . . be here shortly, so we better lose the motor. You go, Cedric. Bring it in the yard, back it into one of the outhouses, take the number plates off.

How do you and Mac get back to the village?

In the boss's motor, growled Cleaver, with the plates from this one. Go on, before he comes and finds us rabbiting – you know what he's like.

The guy called Cedric went out. The other one, Mac, laughed. I hope he gives us time to get well clear of that hall before it goes up, Cave-Troll. There was enough stuff in that holdall to flatten the whole ruddy village.

Cleaver grunted. There's only *some* of it in the hall, you turkey. Rest's hidden around the camp, where the police'll find it. He chuckled. Just in case anybody's in any doubt over who disrupted a public meeting in such a rude manner.

My heart kicked me in the ribs. I gripped my friend's elbow. Asra, I think they've put a bomb in the village hall. My dad . . . half the village'll be there. Your people'll get the blame. We've got to get out, warn everybody.

Asra shook her head. How *can* we, Ruby Tanya? They're at the bottom of the stairs. Anyway, they're your father's friends – why would they—?

225

Ssssh! I hissed. If we could hear them, they could hear us. Window. We'll open a window, climb out. I grabbed both her arms, shook her. I don't *know* why they'd kill Dad, I only know what we just heard. The meeting's in two and a half hours. We've got to do it *now*.

- Ninety
Ruby Tanya

I waited till they were talking, then shoved the door open. Brief squeal. Asra plucked at my jacket. If I go to the village, police will catch me, send me to my country.

I nodded. I know and I'm sorry, but we can't let all those people die. Come on.

We tiptoed across the floor and along the landing to the back of the house. Two bedrooms overlooked a scrapyard of rusting machines, crumpled vehicles and coils of barbed and chicken wire. We took the room to the left, heard Cedric return as we tried the window there. It wouldn't budge. Painted in, I whispered. Come on.

We crossed the landing. If this won't open, I hissed, we'll have to smash it. It was a sash window. We put our palms under the frame and heaved upwards. It slid about ten centimetres with a grinding noise, then jammed. Wait! We strained our ears, but nobody seemed to have heard. I began to wiggle the thing, pushing up at the same time. It rose by microscopic increments, making too much noise in spite of my gentleness. Pity there wasn't a wind, lashing rain, something to mask it.

It took more than five minutes to make a gap high enough to get through. I poked my head out, looking for that convenient fallpipe they always find in stories. It wasn't there – we were in the wrong story. There *was* a wooden lean-to directly under the window, but it was a long drop and you'd probably go through the roof.

I pulled my head in, told Asra. It's not good but it's our only chance. D'you want to go first?

She shook her head. No, I can't. I don't like high. You go, Ruby Tanya.

I can't just *leave* you – there'll be a heck of a crash when I land. They'd have you straight away.

She shook her head again. You go, maybe I will come last.

There wasn't time to argue. I stooped, shoved a leg through and was halfway out when we heard somebody coming upstairs fast. Torn between the need to escape and my love for Asra, I hesitated. Cleaver was on the landing, roaring. Asra screamed. I made a grab for her – we'd fall together – but she resisted and then it was too late. Cave-Troll's massive fist closed on my collar and I was hauled off the sill like a cabbage-patch doll. For a split second his attention was focused on me, and in that second Asra fled. As I writhed, slashing with my nails at the thug's eyes, I saw her hit the stairs running. Go *on*, Asra, I screamed. It's just you now.

I knew these men would kill me: I'd seen and heard too much.

- Ninety-one
Asra

I am running downstairs. At the bottom is two men. I don't
know what I do. I'm so scared. They stand with their arms
spread like goalies; I am the ball. Four steps from the bottom
I throw myself sideways at the banister, roll over it and fall.
It hurts but I bounce up, run to the door. The men are close
behind. It is not *me* running – I am not so fast. It is my fear.
Cold hits me, I am in the yard. The mud slows me but I think
so it slows them more. I am through the gateway, running in
long dead grass. I do not hear their breath now. I look back.
They are standing in the gateway, puffing clouds of that
breath.

Go on, Asra. It's just you now. Last words of Ruby Tanya to
me. Last to anybody, I think so. Cave-Troll Cleaver has her
and it is my fault. My fault. For her I must run to the village,
tell the people, save her father. I head for Mushroom Gap.

At the farm a motor starts. They cannot catch me running,
but with a car . . . I stop, breathing hard, thinking. On Long
Lane they will easily get me, but what if I run to the camp

instead, to Mr Shofiq? Could we then warn the village in time? Will he believe me, when I have hid from police, from my parents? The motor is in the yard, coming out. It is time to decide.

I run over the airfield, towards the camp. I hope so the bad men will think I head for the village, the motor will go to Mushroom Gap. As I run I listen. I hear the motor: it is not closer. I turn, see its lights bounding to the gap. I laugh to myself and run on.

At the camp everything looks the same. I take the path-way to the social club. Mr Shofiq is always there. People stare as I burst in, my hair and clothes are making me look like a wolf girl. I hurry to the office; some of them follow.

Asra? Mr Shofiq's mouth falls open, showing his five teeth. Where have you been? he cries. Everybody is looking for you. I run round the desk, hug his neck and start to cry. The doorway is full of people staring. Go away, shouts Mr Shofiq. All go away. He hugs me, rocks me. All right, he whispers to my ear. It is all right, Asra, you are home.

I start to tell him but he says shush. You are upset, he says, but it is all right. You are just a child, nobody blames you. There is no need to make up stories.

It *isn't* stories, Mr Shofiq, *see.* I dig in my pocket, bring out the plasticine I hid in the wardrobe, put it in his hand. They have many packs of this – it is like bombs. Also they have Ruby Tanya. Cleaver will kill her.

Mr Shofiq looks to me, then to the plasticine in his hand. They have *this*?

They *had* it, at the ruins. Now it is at village hall, also here.

Here?

Hidden, for police to find.

Ah yes, I see. He reaches for the telephone, jabs 999,

says, Police. Then he changes his mind, slams it down. Too slow, he says. You say your friend is at the old farm?

Yes.

How many men?

Three, four maybe.

All right, wait here.

He leaves the office – I never see him move so fast. I look out of the window, thinking about Ruby Tanya. In half a minute he is back. Eight men will go to the farm, he says. They will find your friend. Come with me.

We run outside. The bus is there, its engine running, Mr Malik in the driver's seat. Go! snaps Mr Shofiq as we jump on board. The bus is old, but Mr Malik makes it go faster than he drives to school or the supermarket at Danmouth. Me and Mr Shofiq are flung from side to side as we screech round bends like Michael Schumacher. We hang on. When I dare let go I look at my watch. It is seven o'clock. The meeting will start at half-past. We have a mile to go.

I don't think so we can save them.

– Ninety-two
Ruby Tanya

He slapped me across the head a couple of times, seriously hard slaps that made my ears ring. He'd rake-marks down his cheeks from my nails but I hadn't found his eyes. He half-dangled, half-dragged me downstairs. Mac and Cedric weren't there. I guessed they'd gone after Asra.

Siddown and shuddup. He shoved me towards the chest. Move, and I'll kill you. I believed him, sat stiffly, just breathing. He crossed to the porch doorway and shouted across the yard. What you done with her then? I didn't catch the reply, but Cleaver's bellowed response told me what I desperately wanted to know. Well don't stand there pickin' yer bleat'n snouts: get the motor and go after her.

Asra'd shaken them off, then. It didn't make me feel good, I was much too scared for that, but at least I had the satisfaction of knowing we'd screw up Feltwell's night if Asra made it to the village.

I heard the car start, saw it through the window. It was a van, actually. White van, no lettering on the side. Cleaver watched it go, then came in. She won't get away, he growled, so don't think it. And as for *you*, minute the boss gets here, you're dead. He smiled horribly. In fact you might as well practise while you're waiting. Being dead, I mean.

He rummaged in one of the cardboard boxes, produced a reel of parcel tape and some bubble-wrap. Open wide, he snarled. I opened my mouth and he crammed in the bubble-wrap. I was too terrified to resist, knew that my only chance was Asra. He taped my mouth, then wound the reel round and round my head like he was turning me into a mummy. Panic gripped me. I thought I'd suffocate. I jumped up, moaning and jerking my head from side to side. He slapped me again, spun me round. Hands behind your back, he snapped. Come *on*.

I did what he said and he taped my wrists together, really tight. Then he squatted, pushed up the bottoms of my jeans and bound my ankles, so that I was totally helpless. It wasn't till he raised the lid of the chest that I realized what he'd meant by practising being dead. No! I couldn't *say* that of course; it came out as a muffled hum. I shook my head violently, tears streamed down my cheeks. I even tried to bunny-hop away. I must've looked really pathetic but he didn't care. In fact he was smiling, enjoying himself: I knew for the first time what *merciless* means.

He bent, chucking stuff out of the chest till it was empty. I stood crying, snot and tears running down my chin. He didn't even look at my face, he just scooped me up and dumped me in the chest. I knew, *knew*, I wouldn't get out alive. I did the only thing I could: refused to straighten my legs. My knees jutted above the rim of the chest, the lid rested on them and he couldn't shut it.

It didn't bother Cave-Troll. He raised and slammed the lid

as hard as he could, over and over, till the pain in my kneecaps was worse than my terror and I straightened them in spite of myself. With a shout of triumph he slammed down the lid and plunged me into total darkness.

- Ninety-three
Asra

Mr Malik glances over his shoulder. Where is village hall, please?

Watch the *road*! cries Mr Shofiq, because we are going at sixty miles an hour. Look for Church Lane on the left, he says, just before the green.

It is three minutes past seven as our bus turns left on squealing tyres. Left side, raps Mr Shofiq as we roll up Church Lane, past the church and vicar's house. Mr Malik nods, slams on the brake. We are here. Me and Mr Shofiq pick ourselves up off the floor. Through the window I see the hall, people going in. There are many polices also. When Mr Malik opens the door, a policeman sticks his head in.

In a hurry, are we? he says.

Mr Malik jerks his head to Mr Shofiq and me. *They* are.

Oh, aye? The policeman steps up.

Mr Shofiq goes forward to meet him. There's a bomb, he says, in there. You must get everybody out.

The policeman shakes his head, smiling. You'll have to do

better than that, sunshine. Think I just got off the boat, do you?

Boat? Mr Shofiq frowns. No boat, *bomb*. In the village hall.

Yes, I heard you the first time. Oldest trick in the book, old lad.

Trick?

That's what I said. Oldest trick in the book. Bomb threat, hall evacuated, no meeting, Bob's your uncle.

No! cries Mr Shofiq. We have not come to stop the meeting. We come to warn. There is a—

Please, Mr Policeman. I step forward. I will be caught now, put on a flight to my country, but I can't be silent. I look up to the officer and say, My name is Asra Saber. You have been looking for me. I am living in the ruins. Bad men come, I hide in a wardrobe—

He holds up a hand. I *know*: you go through the wardrobe and find yourself in a strange land, right?

No! what I am telling to you is *true*.

No it's *not*, sweetheart. He sounds tired, turns to Mr Malik. I'm getting off now, he says. I advise you to drive on, turn right and right again: you'll find you're facing the Danmouth road. Stay *here*, you'll find you're facing charges.

He is on the step. Mr Shofiq takes the block of bomb stuff out of his pocket, shows it. D'you know what this is? he asks.

Sure. The officer nods. Plasticine.

It is ten past seven.

- Ninety-four
Ruby Tanya

I tried to concentrate on lying still. Total darkness in a confined space promotes panic, and panic only makes a bad situation worse. You injure yourself thrashing about, and you use more oxygen. I doubted whether the ancient chest was airtight but it *felt* airtight, and my gag added to the feeling of slow suffocation.

So I lay still, breathing slowly. My battered knees prickled; I felt the trickle of blood. The chest wasn't soundproof – I could hear Cleaver moving about, shifting things and muttering to himself. I was listening for the motor which would bring Feltwell. *Minute the boss gets here, you're dead.* Listening for it, praying for it not to come.

It came, after only a few minutes probably, though it felt like hours. I heard the engine die, footfalls in the porch, Feltwell's voice.

What's going on? Where're Mac and Cedric?

Chasing a kid. Other one's in there.

Kid? *What* kid? A scraping noise, the lid was lifted. I

237

gazed up at the face I'd seen at Danmouth mall. Who the heck *is* this? Why's she here?

There were two of 'em, boss, upstairs. Must've been here when we arrived. They were trying to get out through a bedroom window.

You should've *let* them, you idiot. What'm I supposed to do with her, now she's seen my face?

Kill her, boss. Mac'll run the other one over with the van, no danger. Should've done it by now, in fact.

Lovely! And how d'you think we're going to pin two squashed kids on the asylum seekers, you pea-brained tunnel-dwarf?

I . . . dunno, boss. We think they heard us talking, about tonight. Had to do summink.

So you let one of 'em go?

That runaway, Saber. I bet she's been living here.

Feltwell shook his head. You're supposed to have checked the place out *days* ago, you brainless lump. What's the use of me planning everything down to the last detail, if you're going to screw it all up the first time I leave you to do something by yourself? I suppose you're going to tell me next that Mac and Cedric left their mobiles here?

No, boss, they took 'em.

Well, that's something. Get onto them, tell them go to the hall, *whether they found the kid or not*. Got that?

Yes, boss.

Good. And when you've done that, see to this one. And make sure you do a thorough job for once. There's a heavy hammer somewhere about. I'll go do the business.

He left the lid up, went away. I heard a phone beep, Cleaver talking. Feltwell drove off. These were the last moments of my life. I tried not to think about Mum and Gran and Asra; tried not to *think*, but couldn't blank out *heavy hammer*.

And here it came, in Cleaver's giant fist. *Here comes a chopper to chop off your head.* Mum recited that to me once, long ago at bed time. Little did she know. He was smiling, Cleaver. Can you imagine? Looking forward. He walked round the chest, slowly, like a snooker player seeking the best spot, the perfect angle. I closed my eyes.

There came a noise, a scrabbling from the porch, voices shouting. I opened my eyes. Cleaver, hammer raised, mouth open, stared towards the door. In seconds the kitchen filled with men: heaving, grunting men, like a scrum. Cleaver cried out and fell, the hammer rang on the flags. A bearded face looked down at me. Strong arms went under my knees and shoulders. I was scooped out of my coffin.

Out of my *coffin*.

– Ninety-five
Asra

Not plasticine, cries Mr Shofiq; plastic *explosive*, found by this child at the abandoned farm.

For the first time, the policeman seems uncertain. He looks at the bomb stuff, at me, at Mr Shofiq. I . . . hang on a minute, I'll get the sergeant.

It is twelve minutes past seven. People in the queue have noticed who we are, *what* we are. They are casting dirty looks. When the officer goes away, one man runs over and bangs on the side of the bus, shouting bad words. I look down at his face, made ugly by hate. I move away from the window.

Mr Shofiq stands at the door, waiting for the sergeant. Mr Malik is nervous, watching the queue. If these people didn't hate us they wouldn't be here. The man who banged has a group round him now; they keep looking our way. I think so they want to hurt us.

Then I see them. Two men, coming out of the hall. Mac and Cedric. Somebody points to the bus and they look. Our eyes meet and their mouths fall open. I know their secret; they know that I know. I have to be silenced. The angry group is a way to do this. Mac calls to them. Come on, what're we waiting for? Let's *get* 'em.

They are coming towards the bus. I know that if a fight starts, the bomb will explode before the police have time to break it up. There is one thing to do, and one girl to do it. I get up and run down the bus. The men are almost to the door. I push past Mr Shofiq, jump down and run as fast as I can towards the hall. The other men ignore me, but Mac and Cedric break away to chase.

In the entrance a man sits behind a table. Stop her! yells somebody in the queue. The man jumps up and comes round the table, arms spread like a goalie. Again I am the ball. I roll under his table and bounce up facing a long aisle, with row after row of wooden seats to both sides. Most seats have bottoms on them, the place is almost full. At the far end is a platform with a long table. Behind the table are sitting two men. One is Sefton Feltwell, the other must be Ruby Tanya's father. On the wall behind them is a huge banner with the words, BRITAIN FIRST: ALIENS OUT.

People hear the scuffle, turn in their seats, mutter at the alien. If Mac and Cedric are not behind I think so I will run away, but they are close. I run down the aisle; there are five steps to the platform. I clatter up.

Feltwell is on his feet. He recognizes me but not sure what to do. He can't kill me in front of a hundred people. He signals to Mac and Cedric, but they also are not sure. I face my hundred enemies. There is a *bomb*, I cry, same like our school. You must go at once.

Everybody goes quiet, but nobody moves. They are thinking, *This alien thinks we just got off the boat. I* am thinking, *If there's a bomb, why is Feltwell here?*

Ruby Tanya's father stands up, starts to speak. Ladies and gentlemen, my fellow villagers. He looks to me. You see what happens when we let aliens flood in? They don't understand our culture, our traditions, our *democracy*. They think the way to deal with a meeting they don't like is to break it up by scare tactics. By lies. By *verbal terrorism*.

While Mr Redwood is speaking, Feltwell rises quietly and leaves the stage through the curtain. There is clapping, shouts of Yes. All of these people will die, I don't know what to do. I turn to the speaker. Why has Sefton Feltwell left the hall? I ask.

He looks to the empty chair. He is so happy with the shouts and clapping he did not notice. He has no explanation. His silence succeeds where my warning failed. People start looking to one another, murmuring. She should know, says a loud voice. It'll be *her* lot planted it.

This works. Within seconds people are up. Pushing others in their hurry to reach the aisle, which quickly becomes blocked. Chairs fall over, there is jostling, fists fly. Police at the door are trying to get in but the crowd surges, forcing them back. Keep calm, cries an officer. You'll get out quicker. Nobody believes this.

I am watching from the platform, happy these people will not die, unhappy because they think my people are bombers. A hand grips my arm. I cry out, try to pull free. It is Ruby Tanya's father. Come on, he cries. This way. He is pulling me, we go through the curtain and down some wooden steps. It is dark here. I think so he will kill me.

He does not. We hurry along a dim corridor to an open door. He pulls me through the door and we are outside, on the path behind the village hall. There are not many people here. I look to him. Cleaver's got Ruby Tanya, I say.

What? He is hurting my arm.

At the farm. We heard them talking about the village hall. A bomb. We tried to get away but Cleaver came. He grabbed Ruby Tanya, I ran.

Oh, my God! He pulls me towards a corner of the building. Church Lane is full of people hurrying under an orange street lamp. He squeezes my arm, hisses, Don't fight me: if they see you they'll tear you to pieces. In front of us is the car park. We move quickly among the cars. Some are starting up in clouds of exhaust, some moving. People are hurrying to their vehicles. Mr Redwood is hiding me with his body as we pass.

His car is a Volvo. It beeps and flashes as we come near. He opens a door, bundles me in. Keep your head down, he mutters. Some of the people recognize him, he wants to avoid them. He slides in behind the wheel, starts the motor, slams the door. I am lying on the back seat. We move out onto Church Lane. It is stop and start because of other cars. We reach the end, wait, swing right onto the Danmouth road. The driver puts his foot down, the Volvo leaps forward. I hope so we will save Ruby Tanya, and that he does not mean to murder me.

We are almost to the school when the bomb goes off.

– Ninety-six
Asra and Ruby Tanya

It kills nobody, the bomb. The hall empties, then *pouf*! it is gone. Sefton Feltwell does it from the white van, radio signal. He drives away with Mac and Cedric: they think so they have killed everybody.

Yes, and the plan went wrong in other ways too. Like they'd left clues at the scene to make it look as if asylum seekers planted the bomb. Snag was, the guys who saved me from Cave-Troll Cleaver put the frighteners on him and he told them everything: how they broke into the village hall, planted the bomb and scattered the clues; how Feltwell meant to lie low at the Eagle's Nest till the police found the explosives at the camp and lifted the road blocks.

But they can't go back to Eagle's Nest because me and Ruby Tanya knows about it. They think Ruby Tanya is dead but what about me? Did I die in the explosion or not? They are bad men; they don't even go back for Cleaver. They drive the white van into some thick woods to wait till fuss will go away.

Even *that* didn't work: they picked the wrong woods. Turned out it was a bat sanctuary, with a warden and everything. He noticed the van and phoned the police, who picked the three of 'em up less than an hour after the explosion. Unfortunately they came for Dad too. Well, he'd got himself mixed up with those losers, they thought he was one of them.

Monday night I sleep at Ruby Tanya's gran's house. Tuesday is TV peoples everywhere. Me and Ruby Tanya is heroes, they are filming us at school. We go in a van to the ruins. Ruby Tanya has to get in the chest. We miss rehearsals all day.

Wednesday's papers were full of it. NAZI BOMB PLOT FOILED was one headline; BF FRAME-UP FAILS was another. No prizes for guessing who came up with KIDS' KOOL KOURAGE KRACKS KONSPIRACY. Dad was released without charge that day too, which was a relief to all concerned.

Bestest bits come later though. I am still with Ruby Tanya's gran. No police come to take me away. Friday, editor Hadwin of the *Star* is writing that I must not be sent to my country because I save many lifes. Next day, other papers are saying the same.

And it gets better. After Hadwin's piece, people started bombarding the *Star* with letters and faxes and e-mails, demanding not only that Asra should be allowed to settle in England, but that her *parents* be brought back too. These were villagers, the same people who'd flocked to hear Dad speak out against asylum seekers. It was unbelievable.

The spirit of reconciliation even spread to school. The bullying stopped, and the name-calling. One break time Shazad Butt knocked on Ramsden's door and confessed he'd

245

stuck the blades through Allardyce's trainers. The head gave him a terrific telling-off – you could hear him in the yard – but he didn't expel him. Allardyce responded the same day, admitting he'd put Asif Akhtar in hospital. Amazing.

Amazing, yes, and I am every day having presents in the post from peoples I do not know. Gran says her house is getting like a shop. I think so it is because of Christmas, but Christmas comes and goes and the presents do not stop.

Halfway through January, a letter came to Gran's from the government. It was for Asra, to say she might settle in England if somebody would take responsibility for her. Gran wrote straight back saying she'd be that somebody. She threw a party to celebrate, and *Dad* came. I could hardly believe it, and that wasn't all. Bring fireworks, Gran said when he told her he'd be there, and he said, *No: there's been enough explosions in Tipton Lacey*. You should've seen Mum's face.

I've made it up with Millie, by the way. Told her I was sorry I'd used her as an alibi without asking. I *was* too, when I took the time to think about it. She didn't exactly throw herself at me, but bit by bit it's come all right between us. I've got *two* best friends now: no law against it, is there?

And they all lived happily ever after. Well, no, not *all*. Sefton Feltwell's doing fifteen years in a prison his company built. It's rubbish, four years old and leaks like a sieve. Hardly anything works. The staff hate it, but they know who's to blame so that's all right.

Anything else? Oh yes: the Sabers aren't back yet, but the campaign's gathering strength. Asra reckons her family'll be together again quite soon.

Snug as a bug in a rug.

ABOUT THE AUTHOR

Robert Swindells left school at fifteen and worked as a copyholder on a local newspaper. At seventeen he joined the RAF for three years, two of which he served in Germany. He then worked as a clerk, an engineer and a printer before training and working as a teacher. He is now a full-time writer and lives on the Yorkshire moors.

He has written many books for young readers. *Room 13* won the 1990 Children's Book Award. *Abomination* won the 1999 Stockport Children's Book Award and was shortlisted for the Whitbread Prize, the Sheffield Children's Book Award, the Lancashire Children's Book Award *and* the 1999 Children's Book Award. His books for older readers include *Stone Cold,* which won the 1994 Carnegie Medal, as well as the award-winning *Brother in the Land.* As well as writing, Robert Swindells enjoys keeping fit, travelling and reading.

Blitzed

Robert Swindells

Imagine being alive before your parents were even born!

George is fascinated by World War Two - bombers, Nazis, doodlebugs. Even evacuation and rationing has got to be more exciting than living in dreary old Witchfield! He is looking forward to his school trip to Eden Camp, a World War Two museum. But he doesn't realize quite how authentic this visit to wartime Britain will be . . .

A hand reaching out of the fake rubble, a slip in time, and George has to survive something much worse than boredom. The rubble is now *real* – he has slipped through time into 1940s London!

A thrilling drama from a master of suspense, Robert Swindells.

'A first-rate time-travel story . . . Swindells is a powerful, thrilling writer . . . as good as Robert Westall's classic, *The Machine Gunners*.' INDEPENDENT ON SUNDAY

'Entertaining and thought-provoking . . . has a wonderfully satisfying ending' THE BOOKSELLER

ISBN 0 440 86397 X

ABOMINATION

Robert Swindells

**Martha is twelve, and very different from other kids.
No TV. No computer. No cool clothes.
Especially, no *friends*.**

**It's all because of her parents. Strict members of a
religious group, their rules dominate Martha's life.
But one rule is the most important of all: Martha
must never *ever* invite anyone home. If she does,
their terrible secret – Abomination –
could be revealed . . .**

'A taut and thrilling novel from a master of
the unpredictable' DAILY TELEGRAPH

WINNER OF THE 1999 STOCKPORT CHILDREN'S BOOK AWARD

WINNER OF THE 1999 SHEFFIELD CHILDREN'S BOOK AWARD

SHORTLISTED FOR THE WHITBREAD PRIZE,
THE LANCASHIRE CHILDREN'S BOOK AWARD
and THE 1999 CHILDREN'S BOOK AWARD

ISBN 0 440 86362 7

INVISIBLE!

Robert Swindells

What would *you* do if you could become invisible?

**Creep around, unseen? Listen in to other
people's conversations? Twins Carrie and Conrad,
and their friends Peter and Charlotte do all
these things, and much more, when a new girl
at school – Rosie – shows them her secret:
how to make yourself invisible.**

**It's exciting, and it's fun. It can also be frightening . . .
and dangerous. Especially when Rosie's dad
becomes a suspect in a local crime and the gang
go invisible to find the real crooks . . .**

A gripping adventure from a master of suspense, author of
the award-winning *Room 13* and many other titles.

'Robert Swindells writes the kinds of books that are so scary
you're afraid to turn the page' YOUNG TELEGRAPH

ISBN 0 440 86363 5